"THERE'S BEEN A TERRIBLE ACCIDENT."

As she spoke, Mommy's eyes didn't seem to be able to land anywhere, particularly not on Jessica Ann, whose own eyes widened with alarm even as her heart began to race.

"When I went to speak to Mrs. Withers, she was lying on the floor..." Mommy gestured with a graceful open hand, her brow furrowing gravely as she seemed to be picturing the image as she described it to her daughter. "...she'd been up a ladder, decorating the room for you children."

"Oh, Mommy," Jessica Ann said. "Oh no..."

Mommy nodded and looked skyward, reflectively. "She must have been a very...*thoughtful* teacher."

Jessica Ann felt as if she'd been hit in the pit of her stomach. "Mommy, you make it sound like she's..."

"Dead," Mommy said. "Yes, she's dead, dear."

Numbing shock hit Jessica Ann in a wave.

Mommy was shrugging, saying, "I think she may have broken her neck."

MOMMY

MAX ALLAN COLLINS

LEISURE BOOKS  NEW YORK CITY

For Patty McCormack

A LEISURE BOOK®

November 1997

Published by

Dorchester Publishing Co., Inc.
276 Fifth Avenue
New York, NY 10001

ISBN 0-8439-4322-X

Printed in the United States of America.

"It seemed to her suddenly that violence was an inescapable factor of the heart...an ineradicable thing that lay, like a bad seed, behind kindness, behind compassion, behind the embrace of love itself."

—William March

a short story

by Max Allan Collins

Chapter One

Mommy cried at Mr. Sterling's funeral, but Jessica Ann was pretty sure she was faking. The child had only the vaguest memory of her father's funeral—Jessica Ann had been only six then, whereas now she was a worldly ten—but that memory did include tears forming in those beautiful china blue eyes, rolling down Mommy's lovely face, those perfectly chiseled features framed by blades of ice-blond hair.

Only now, looking back as best she could, Jessica Ann had to wonder—was the memory false? Had Mommy been faking then, too?

Sitting next to her mother in the church pew, Jessica Ann was a petite echo of Mommy, even down to the simple dignified black dress with black nylons. Mommy had never let Jessica Ann wear nylons before; in fact, Jessica Ann was sometimes embarrassed by how "little girl" the clothing was that her Mommy bought for her. The child had almost no say in such matters.

Of course Mommy also had a pillbox hat and a veil, which Jessica Ann did not.

She felt a hand slip into hers and squeeze, comfortingly. Not Mommy's hand, of course—that wasn't Mommy's way. It was Aunt Beth, seated on Jessica Ann's other side, smiling down bravely at her. With her other hand, Aunt Beth clutched a tissue, which she dabbed at her eyes.

Aunt Beth's tears weren't faked. Not that she had been close to Mr. Sterling, but Aunt Beth was just that kind of person. She was very different from Mommy.

Funny thing was, she was just as attractive, in her way, as Mommy. Younger than Mommy, Aunt Beth had hair that was deep brown and very long, though she usually kept it tucked up in a bun. Though she wore almost no makeup, she had really pretty features—great big luminous brown eyes, cheekbones like a model. Even Mommy knew it.

"I'd kill for your complexion," Mommy had told her once. "If you'd just get your nose fixed, you could do much better than Robert."

Jessica Ann didn't see anything wrong with Aunt Beth's nose, but Mommy was right about Uncle Bob. "Robert" was how Mommy always referred to Uncle Bob, who Aunt Beth had recently divorced. Uncle Bob ran a garage—he didn't own it, but she'd heard Aunt Beth tell Mommy, "He makes good money." Mommy never liked him, telling Aunt Beth, "Can't you do better than some grease monkey you picked up in a bar?"

Actually, Uncle Bob had always been nice to Jessica Ann, but the child had seen things. Like at Thanksgiving when Uncle Bob got really drunk and started shouting and the Sterlings had to leave. Like the two times Aunt Beth showed up in the middle of the night, once with her nose bloody, the other time with her eye all puffy and swollen.

In situations like that, Mommy was wonderful. She would put her arm around Aunt Beth—something Mommy *rarely* did—and guide her to the living room couch. Mommy seemed genuinely angry about what happened to Aunt Beth, in that cold way of hers.

"Somebody ought to do something about that bastard," she had said.

Mommy almost never swore, at least not in front of Jessica Ann.

"He can't help it," Aunt Beth said, sniffling, holding onto Mommy tight. "It's his drinking. It's a sickness."

"I know a cure," Mommy said, but didn't say what it was.

The first time it happened, Mr. Sterling was home, and he got mad, too, but not cold mad like Mommy; his face got red as a party balloon and he put his coat on over his jammies and went over and "read that son of a bitch the riot act."

Mr. Sterling swore a little more than Mommy.

The second time it happened, Mr. Sterling was away on business, and it was just the three girls, Mommy, Aunt Beth, and Jessica Ann, on the couch together, with Aunt Beth's eye turning black and swelling shut.

Mommy's upper lip was quivering, just a little. She said, "What makes him think he can get away with hurting my sister?"

Aunt Beth stayed over that night, in the guest room. Mommy wouldn't let her go back to that house.

The problem was, Aunt Beth always forgave Uncle Bob. When he sobered up, he would act nice and say he was sorry—maybe he *was* sorry. That second time, he seemed really sorry. He seemed—what was the word Mommy used?—*contrite*, when they visited him in the hospital.

That second time he beat on Aunt Beth, he'd got so drunk afterward, he'd fallen down the steps and broken his leg.

Bob seemed surprised to see Mommy and Jessica Ann come visit him in the hospital. He was a big man with light brown hair and was what you'd call "ruggedly handsome" except that his eyebrows were too shaggy and a few gross hairs grew out of his nostrils. His broken leg in its big cast was in the air on a pulley contraption, like he'd had a skiing accident or something.

Under the shaggy brows, his eyes were big. His words were a funny combination of anger and fear: "What are *you* doing here?"

"Paying our respects," Mommy said.

From behind her back, Jessica Ann held out the blood-red flowers in the little vase. Mommy patted Jessica Ann's shoulder and said, "Put them on his nightstand, dear."

She did.

"That should cheer you up," Mommy said.

"Th-thanks," he said.

Then Mommy just smiled at him, a placid sort of smile with no teeth showing.

Bob swallowed and said, "I swear, I . . . I'll never do it again."

"Beth is going to ask you for a divorce. Don't contest it."

"I . . . I can't get a divorce. I'm a Catholic."

"Ah. Original sin. Interesting doctrine. Beth and I, our family, we're Baptists, going way back." She made a *tch-tch* sound in her cheek. "I always thought my father was a little stuffy in his opposition to interfaith marriages . . . till now."

Uncle Bob had an alarmed expression. "I'd be excommunicated. . . ."

"You know, Robert, if I might make another suggestion—you really should consider Alcoholics Anonymous." She shook her head and her voice sounded really concerned. "Your next drunken fall could be your last. Where would you end up? Purgatory?"

It seemed so funny, a big man like Uncle Bob, shaking like that. He must have been sicker than Jessica Ann thought.

Later, at home, sitting at the kitchen table with Mommy, Jessica Ann asked how exactly Uncle Bob had gotten hurt. And Mommy said Uncle Bob told the police he heard an intruder downstairs—the bedroom was on the second floor—and woke up to check it out.

"Then in his drunken stupor he tripped and fell a full flight," Mommy said, her coffee cup poised beneath the thin line of her little smile.

"That's terrible," Jessica Ann had said, and sipped her cocoa.

"Terrible he didn't break his neck." Then Mommy looked at her and the cold mean mask of her face melted into a warm smile. "Of course I don't mean that, dear. But you know, I love your Aunt Beth very much."

"Yes, Mommy."

"And I don't like seeing anyone hurt my baby sister."

"Yes, Mommy."

But Mommy had a funny way, sometimes, of showing Aunt Beth she cared. Like criticizing her clothes for being too casual. Like telling her she was skinny and should eat more, but then when she gained weight, suggesting a liquid diet. Or like complaining that a woman with a college education, a teaching degree, was wasting herself working at a preschool.

"You simply must build up your self-esteem, dear," Mommy would tell Aunt Beth.

As an only child, Jessica Ann didn't understand,

couldn't imagine, what having sisters or brothers would be like. But it must have been special. Because Mommy and Aunt Beth, if they weren't related, would never have spent so much time together. They would never have been friends. Yet blood made them more.

Mr. Sterling looked handsome in the coffin, at visitation at the funeral home last night. "He looks like he's sleeping," people said, and they were right. He had a peaceful little smile. Eyes closed. The makeup on his face was a little fake, but it didn't disturb Jessica Ann seeing him like that. He looked a lot better than he had on the stretcher in the middle of the night after his heart attack.

Now it was closed, the coffin, and the white-haired minister was talking about shepherds and sheep in a rumbly but soothing voice. The words didn't seem to have anything special to do with Mr. Sterling, and they became a blur, a sound, nothing specific, like Mommy's noisy dishwasher before she got it fixed, only louder.

Jessica Ann did hear him say something about Mr. Sterling having a lot of friends, and he *did*, too—this great big church was filled with people. Old people, like Mr. Sterling, who was a lot older than Mommy, twenty years older—he was sixty when he died, the papers said.

Did they think about dying, she wondered, these old people? When an old person went to a funeral of a friend, was it terrible, knowing they might be next?

It was a question her mind was nimble enough to ask, but unable to grapple with, for to Jessica Ann—like to any child—her life was an endless road stretching before her. A funeral wasn't a reminder of the fragility of life and the inevitably of death; it was just an odd grown-up ritual that seemed sad and somber and not that much different from a Sunday morning church service, except that church on Sunday wasn't spooky.

This was like a church service combined with one of those black-and-white monster movies—*Dracula, Frankenstein, The Mummy*!—she and Aunt Beth watched late at night, sometimes, when Mommy and Mr. Sterling went out on a "date."

This church wasn't the one she and her mother normally went to; this was the First Methodist, and was bigger and brighter than Second Calvary, where Mommy took her for Sunday school and church. Mr. Sterling had switched over to Mommy's church after they got married, in fact they got married at Second Calvary; and Mommy was irritated when the instructions among Mr. Sterling's papers specified that his funeral be held at First Methodist.

Aunt Beth said that was because it was the church where his children by his second wife (Mommy was his third) had gone. At visitation last night, Jessica Ann had met those "children" for the first time, and they were adults! Every time she'd heard Mommy or Mr. Sterling refer to them, they were "children" or "the kids," and they turn out to be a man who had to be at least thirty and a woman who was even older!

They seemed nice enough—the girl, or the woman, was named Alice and the boy, the man, was named Jerome. Alice looked a little like Mr. Sterling, only pretty, and Jerome didn't look like anybody. Alice was a redheaded lady, a little overweight, with a husband who was a lot overweight, and Jerome was thin with a thin mustache and no tie and no wife.

Mommy told Aunt Beth that Jerome was "from San Francisco," and raised her eyebrows and rolled her eyes. Jessica Ann wondered if there was something wrong with being from San Francisco.

Anyway, this was the church that Mr. Sterling's "kids" had gone to, and Jessica Ann thought—spooky funeral service or not—it was very beautiful. The pews were a golden brown, not the dark dark brown of Second Calvary; the walls were a pale pale green, a big white cross hung from chains suspended over the altar (was that dangerous?), and behind the altar curved the pipes of a massive organ, like a big weird silver smile.

Most of all, Jessica Ann was struck by the beauty of the looming stained glass windows on either side of the sanctuary. Her church had stained glass windows, too, but just designs with Bible sayings in that old-time lettering. They didn't depict scenes like these lovely paintings of glass.

At left, under a purple sky, Jesus in flowing green robes approached a woman in yellow who sat weeping on some broken stones at the unsealed tomb. She looked sad, as sad as Mr. Sterling's children did right now; only Mr. Sterling wasn't exactly going to surprise them by walking up behind them with the news of his resurrection.

The window at right showed the baby Jesus being presented to the kneeling wise men by Jesus's mother, Mary, while Joseph looked proudly on. The panes of the other window, which was sort of an Easter window after all, were green and gold and copper. This was more of a Christmas window, and there were reds and deep blues and deep greens, and the wise men were dressed so colorfully.

And Jesus's mother had the most serene, lovely face. Jessica Ann looked up at Mommy and was not surprised to see that Mommy's face looked just that very way.

Late afternoon sunlight was filtering in the Easter window, painting the sanctuary and its pews and its people peaceful hues of copper and gold. But the Christmas window was the one people would look up at, stealing looks, sometimes gazing, their sad faces reflective, meditative.

After all, Christmas was only a few days away.

Aunt Beth said it was too bad Mr. Sterling had to die at this time of year. But Mommy said she thought that was a good thing, a nice thing.

"Every Christmas," Mommy said, "we'll be reminded of him. He'll live on in our hearts and memories."

That was a warm thing to say, but somehow when Mommy said it, it came out chilly.

Not as chilly as the cemetery, though, where the recent snowfall made walking hazardous for the old people headed for the graveside, the men holding onto the women as if to help them not fall but really to keep from falling themselves.

Jessica Ann held Mommy's hand as they walked, and Mommy's grasp was cool—Mommy was wearing black leather gloves. They sat on folding chairs on a little astro-turf rug under a canopy while the white-haired minister spoke again. There were more people than the chairs could accommodate—Mr. Sterling had a *lot* of friends—and the setting sun dappled everything gold and copper, again, like in church.

And, again, the drone of the minister's voice never quite turned into words for the girl; she was looking at the tombstones rising out of the white snow like perfect little buildings, throwing long tall shadows as the golden hues gave way to a cool blue of twilight. Mr. Sterling's gleaming silver coffin was lowered into the ground and it caught glints of the dying sun.

At the house, there was a kind of party, which struck Jessica Ann as awfully strange. She loved their house on Rockwell Road. It was a big tan two-story house that looked like it had been built a long time ago, but was really pretty new. A "modern Victorian," was how Mommy described it. The big house stood on a small yard on the corner of a cul-de-sac in the Woodcreek development. They'd lived here for a year and a half, ever since Mommy married Mr. Sterling.

This was the most people Jessica Ann had ever seen in the house. Mommy didn't like big parties, at least not big parties in *her* house. But apparently, after a funeral, you had to feed the dead person's friends.

Aunt Beth was busy behind the big counter in the blindingly white kitchen, working with some older lady relatives of Mr. Sterling's. (Both Mommy's parents were dead. Jessica Ann didn't think of them as "grandma and grandpa" because they had died before she was born.) They weren't cooking, out in the kitchen, just dealing with food people had brought, covered dishes and salads and deviled eggs and pies and cakes and cookies. It was definitely the biggest party ever at the Sterling house.

Almost like a Christmas party, with the beautifully trimmed tall tree in the front window. The plastic pine arrayed with white china cherubs ribboned with red (last year, Mommy's theme was blue stars and suns and moons) was the only concession to the season Mommy made; she didn't like spoiling the interior decorating she'd personally supervised with a lot of cheap clutter.

Mommy didn't like clutter. Magazines didn't sit out in the Sterling house, not even *TV Guide*. No wall bore more than one framed picture—these were prints chosen to color coordinate with the rose and turquoise furnishings and draperies—and every piece of furniture was both functional and tasteful. No bric-a-brac or knickknacks or mementos sat out—unless you counted family portraits—in the very modern interior of the old-fashioned house with its stark white walls. What a refreshing change to have this immaculate place cluttered up with people for once—even if it did take a funeral to do it.

But Jessica Ann was the only kid, and it got boring real fast, old people standing in little groups, talking in hushed voices while they nibbled at plates of food and sipped at cups of coffee. Some went out to smoke on the open cement porch that wrapped around half of the house.

Mommy sat in the living room, in a regal easy chair that had been bought for its looks not comfort (that was the child's theory, at least). The chair was fairly near the front door, separated by a waist-high divider on which the phone perched, and from this position Mommy could greet and bid farewell to her guests. Everybody came around and paid their respects and Mommy just smiled and nodded bravely and said nice things about Mr. Sterling, like a queen receiving her court, one at a time.

Funny thing—Mr. Sterling's "kids" didn't come to the party. Maybe they had to head home—they didn't live in Ferndale, anymore, after all. Maybe they had airplanes to catch, or long drives to start.

Jessica Ann sat in the kitchen for a while, at the table (every chair in the living room was taken, sofa, too), where all the food was spread out; but she soon got tired of the traffic. Funerals apparently made people hungry, because some of the guests, the men particularly, kept coming back for more.

She went to her mommy, quietly waiting for the latest guest to express their sorrow and move on; the child sat on the arm of Mommy's chair and whispered, "Can I go upstairs to my room, Mommy?"

"You've been such a good girl, today." Mommy stroked Jessica Ann's cheek with her forefinger; this was, coming from Mommy, quite a demonstrative gesture. Then, though still seated, Mommy tucked her hands behind her back, clasping them there. "Who's your best friend?"

"You are, Mommy," Jessica Ann said, feeling a warm rush that rarely if ever accompanied this ritual between them, which dated before the beginning of the child's memory.

Mommy placed a hand over her own heart. "Who loves you more than anything on God's green earth?"

"You do, Mommy."

Mommy smiled and brushed the air with a dismissive little wave. "Run along, then, dear," Mommy said. "Go on up, and read your books and listen to your CDs. Just don't turn the music up too loud."

Which was silly, because all the hushed talking was adding up to a real racket; but Jessica Ann just smiled, kissed her mother on the cheek, said, "Yes, Mommy," and went up the stairs to her room.

Chapter Two

Beth wasn't worried about her sister; her sister could take care of herself.

In fact, Phillip Sterling's widow was in her element in the aftermath of her husband's middle-of-the-night coronary. She had administered CPR. She had summoned the proper mix of controlled hysteria (for the 911 call), near-tearful concern (for the paramedics), and finally dazed grief (at the emergency room where her husband was pronounced DOA). She had handled the funeral arrangements with enviable grace and military precision.

Now, at the postfuneral gathering at the Sterling home, Beth's sister was truly in peak form. As Beth scurried from the kitchen to the living and dining rooms, gathering dirty dishes and empty cups (no paper plates in the *Sterling* household!), blowing away tendrils of pinned-back hair that snaked down to tickle and tease her, sweat dampening and staining the underarms of her gray silk blouse (despite her best Dry Idea defenses), Beth would catch glimpses of her sister, her perfect sister.

Perfectly coiffed, every icy platinum hair in place, her lovely legs sleek and strong in sheer black nylon, knees together, ankles together, hands clasped in her lap; she might have been a schoolgirl, so proper and prim was her posture—the teacher's pet. With that nobly suffering expression, she would accept the offered hands of sympathy, narrowing her eyes with just the right amount of sorrow and wisdom, shaking her head the same way, smiling a brave closed-mouth smile (she would be careful not to show any teeth—that perfect dazzling smile could never be properly adjusted to sorrow level). She was holding back the anguish of losing "her beloved Phillip" with such exquisite bearing, such unerring dignity.

The question Beth had never been able to answer about her sister, a question that had haunted her since childhood, was simply this: Was the woman repressing deep feelings that she only allowed the world glimpses of (at proper occasions, such as this one); or did she feel little or nothing at all, and were these merely expected, expertly manufactured responses?

To characterize her sister as emotionless would be too easy, not to mention inaccurate. Beth well-remembered the violent childhood rages that manifested themselves on the rare occasions her sister had not gotten her way; Beth, two years younger, had watched her sister develop certain skills that kept a fiery temper at bay. The child had learned early on that her lovely smile and her charming, precocious, oddly formal mastery of the English language could get her more from grown-ups than temper tantrums; and in her teenage years, Beth's sister had combined girlish charm with womanly attributes to get her way from both Daddy and a long succession of boyfriends.

The rest of the family wasn't really fooled by the girl's contrived charisma. She'd had a special place in Daddy's heart because she was the firstborn, and the only child by his first wife, who had died under tragic circumstances that were never discussed. And she was a lovely child, apparently the image of her late mother, and a brilliant student, with an exceptional IQ.

But Mom never warmed to the child—though she often pretended to love the girl, for Daddy's sake, even aiding and abetting his "spoiling" her—and at best mother and stepdaughter had maintained a chilly truce. Daddy had been a lot older than Mom—he was a retired military man—and Beth supposed that her sister's penchant for older men, like Mr. Sterling and Jessica Ann's late father, had something to do with that.

Even in high school terms, the girl had chosen "older" boys. Funny to look back at Chad Harrison and realize that Ferndale Senior High's towering, brawny All-Conference quarterback had only been a kid, eighteen. But her sister had only been fourteen, a ninth-grader to Chad's Most Popular Senior Boy, and that had formed an enormous gulf understandable even now.

To look at her this evening, that proper widow who had so carefully constructed a country-club, society-page life for herself, it seemed almost absurd to remember that once upon a time she'd been the youngest girl on the Varsity cheerleading squad, that the platinum blond hair had been a golden shower of curls on the shoulders of a body that every girl in school coveted and every boy craved.

But Beth—unlike her younger brother Steven and little sis Cindy, whose absence at the funeral today spoke volumes of their disdain for their older half sister—could find compassion for her father's darling. She knew that Daddy's death, an aneurysm that took him from his loving family in the midst of a family vacation, had sent her big sister reeling.

Daddy had been her world. Daddy may have been the only creature on earth the girl truly loved, other then herself. Add to this Mom's new, more openly hostile treatment of the household's former favorite, and Beth could easily understand why her sister would set her sights on the likes of a Chad Harrison.

Who wouldn't? Chad looked like Robert Redford, except for his eyes being closer together, and even if he wasn't really very bright, he had a rosy future ahead as a local athlete with a Big Ten scholarship waiting. Plus, his father owned the biggest Pontiac/

Cadillac dealership in the state, and Chad was an only child.

He was the biggest catch at Ferndale High, and she caught him, all right. Beth never found out exactly what happened, but her best guess was that her sister told Chad she was pregnant, prompting him to drive her across three state lines to where they could get married without a blood test. Chad was no reluctant groom, however. Beth knew that much firsthand.

Beth had always gotten along with her sister's boyfriends; they seemed to gravitate to her, adopting her as a kid sister. In retrospect, she realized they were getting a kind of understanding, friendly ear, and even companionship from her that her sister couldn't provide. She had a hunch her sister was wonderful company—whether in the backseat of a Chevy or on the dance floor at a sock hop—but not really somebody you could sit down and talk to.

She and Chad, for example, used to sit and talk and talk. Beth had a terrible crush on him, and wondered if he ever guessed, and if he ever thought of her as anything but a surrogate sister. But who could look from her golden-haired shapely cheerleader sister to her—flat-chested, scrawny bookworm seventh-grader with a nose that would frighten birds away—and think of anything but the cheerleader?

"I'm crazy about her," Chad told Beth one afternoon, about a month before the elopement. "She's the most beautiful girl in the world, and so God-awful smart."

With the exception of math (always a blind spot for Beth) her grades were actually just as good as her sister's.

Beth had said, "You're the first boy she's ever gotten really serious about."

"I know," he said, and looked away, almost blushing.

Beth was pretty sure Chad had taken her sister's virginity; it had only been after Daddy's death that birth control pills made a regular appearance in her sister's purse.

"You know," Chad said, "you can be married and go to college, too."

"You're not thinking of getting married, are you? She's just a ninth-grader. . . . Ninth-graders don't get married."

"Fourteen-year-olds can marry in some states," he said. "Some states, it's even younger."

"Who told you that?"

He shrugged. "It's not important." Then he looked up; he was so cute, that straw-colored Redford bang brushing his freckled forehead. "But I'd have my scholarship, and I bet my folks would help us out. . . ."

"This is crazy, Chad. She's got your ring. Isn't that enough?"

His eyes were so earnest she had to look away as he said, "Do you think she'd wait for me?"

Beth hadn't known what to say. She almost

blurted, "Sure, unless something better comes along." Instead, she just said, "She's never been more serious about anybody."

And Chad had nodded and smiled and his eyes got very tight, moving quickly, side to side, in tortured thought.

When the happy couple returned to announce their state of wedded bliss to Chad's folks, the excrement had hit the rotary blades. The Harrisons were embarrassed and devastated, but it was Mom who had gone truly ballistic, making noises about "statutory rape." Mom and Beth's sister had some screaming matches behind closed bedroom doors, and during one, the sound of a slap had rung out, startling the three kids eavesdropping in the hall; they had gone scurrying like cockroaches to their holes, though the major topic of discussion thereafter was who slapped who. . . .

Somehow the ill-fated "marriage" was kept very quiet, though there were rumblings around school. Beth wasn't privy to the details—and her sister had withdrawn into a glacial state of rage—but Beth gathered that there was no real pregnancy, and the marriage was promptly annulled, and Chad was grounded for the remainder of his senior year, finally being allowed to go to the prom (not with Beth's sister, of course). Mom was looking into a private school out east for her wayward stepdaughter.

The following summer, when the house burned down, Mom was the only one killed. Beth and her sister—who had awoken her with untypical hysteria ("I smell smoke! It's a *fire*, I tell you!")—had rounded up their brother and sister and they got out a second-floor window to a partial roof from which they could lower themselves to the yard. The stairway to the attic, which Mom and Dad had remodeled into a master bedroom after Cindy came along, had been a sea of flames none of them dared try to navigate.

But they had heard their mother, heard her screaming. The screams seemed faint over the sound of devouring flames, flames that were turning their white frame house orange and blue and red and black, with gray-black smoke fluming skyward, mushroom-clouding around the house as if to protect it, as if to shield it, further muffling the screams of a woman within, screams that seemed more echoes of screams than screams, as the four children below huddled together in two hugging pairs, Steven and Cindy grasping each other, screaming as if in reply to their mother, while the older girls clutched each other silently, anguished tears streaming down Beth's face, while her sister, the older child, the one in charge, the one who had saved them all, who the papers and TV and radio would praise, looked up at the black windows with pinched features and dry eyes that might have been a brave repressing of pain, or just a pensive expression mitigated by smoke.

Dad's sister Clara, who was what they used to call "a maiden lady," took the four children into her house; it was a duplex, half of which Clara rented out. Soon the entire house was converted to a single family dwelling, and the four kids—each in their own way—ran roughshod over the sweet plump good-natured old woman. In particular, Steven and Cindy had been wild teenagers, though Cindy straightened out (she was a psychologist in Seattle), while Steven—a talented blues guitarist—had gotten seriously into drugs and to this day was in and out of rehab centers; currently he was working as an assistant manager at a used CD shop in Atlanta.

Beth and Aunt Clara got along fine, but Beth went her own way, ignoring the old woman's house rules. In her sophomore year, Beth started "dating" and the boys she dated weren't always the best choices. She had a fake ID and looked mature in makeup and hit the singles scene pretty hard. During her senior year, a time that embarrassed her to think about now, she partied every weekend; she didn't hit the metal bars like most girls in her crowd, but rather the "meat market" discos. She used to joke that she may not have been a raving beauty, "but I clean up good," and in truth, with her long brown hair down and a decent application of mascara and lipstick, she could do pretty well for herself—if you considered one-night stands with mostly married men doing pretty well for yourself. After an AIDS scare, she straightened out in college, but her recent marriage to Bob indicated she still had a tendency toward the wrong kind of man.

"I like 'em dumb and pretty and mean," she said once, well into her cups, to a girlfriend whose reply had been, "Truer words were never spoken, honey."

Of course, Aunt Clara had loved and doted upon the older girl. Clara knew nothing of the annulled marriage; Clara saw and knew only the well-behaved, polite, lovely Honor Roll student who had national honors in cheerleading competition. It was no surprise that when Clara died, shortly after Cindy graduated high school, the old woman's estate went largely to the oldest girl, including the house. Mom's estate had set up trust funds that looked after the rest of the kids, though, and there had been college money for all of them.

Beth knew her sister's lack of real tears at her husband's funeral was pretty much par for the course. What disturbed her was Jessica Ann's similar, seemingly impassive reaction.

The child had always had a natural sensitivity; she was born with a good heart. But Beth was worried for Jessy, because didn't any child learn from the example of their parents? And what if this sweet, compassionate little girl was learning from her mommy that it was only proper to repress emotions, and that public displays of emotion and/or affection were in fact improper? What if the seed of goodness within this child came to be covered with a hard shell of emotionless restraint?

When all but a few guests had left, with Mr. Sterling's two sisters busy taking care of the dishes, Beth slipped up the stairs, pausing at the landing to look back at her sister, still holding court; the woman's eyes were on her, those beautiful sky-blue eyes frozen in their unblinking sockets, laser-beaming up at her, and the careful veil of grief she wore slipped away for a moment into that accusing expression Beth knew all too well.

Beth's sister did not like her interfering with the way she was raising Jessica Ann; this had been made clear to Beth, many times.

Nervously, Beth leaned over the landing rail and stage-whispered, "I'm just going to see how Jessica Ann is holding up under the strain."

And her sister's eyes softened and for the first time this afternoon the dazzling smile—with those blindingly white teeth—made an appearance.

"Thank you, Beth," she said. "That's sweet of you."

And Beth had smiled, surprised by the small leap of relief and joy she felt within her; why, after all these years, did her sister's sanction mean so much? Why did she so eagerly lap up the few meager morsels of affection that her sister bestowed?

Padding soundlessly down the carpeted hall, taking the turn to the child's room, Beth paused and knocked on the door, then cracked it open and peeked in, looking toward the left where the girl's bed extended from the wall, with a whispered, "Busy in there?"

The child had changed her clothes, from the black mourning dress that echoed her mommy's into a little pink and white sweater-top with tiny cloth flowers and denim pants with rhinestones, as close to casual an outfit as her mother allowed. She lay on top of the pastel green bedspread on the antique white four-poster, reading an R. L. Stine *Goosebumps* book, with her collection of stuffed toys pushed to one side of her, stuffed animals mostly (her mommy wouldn't allow her any real pets), with one pointy-hatted white-faced blue clown the apparent ringmaster.

Jessica Ann's eyes crinkled and so did her chin as she said, "You won't tell Mommy . . ."

The child was referring to the scary book, which was definitely not on Mommy's approved reading list.

"Of course not, Jessy," Beth said, sitting on the edge of the bed.

Tucking the book beneath her floral-patterned pillow, the child smiled, partly in relief, partly (Beth thought) because she liked it when her aunt called her "Jessy." Beth was the only one who called her that; it was a private symbol of the special relationship they shared.

The bedroom was the largest in the house and was overseen by a lovely half-circle window whose three panes made a decorative pattern on the wall as moon- and streetlights shone in. Beth had never quite figured out why her sister had given the girl such a choice room, one that had clearly been designed to be the master bedroom—it wasn't like the woman to be unselfish, after all—but then in a very real way, the room wasn't Jessica Ann's, was it?

Even though they had lived in a nice house, a large two-story house, with four kids in the family, three of them girls, it was inevitable that Beth and her sister be thrown into a bedroom together. This had happened around the sixth grade, and Beth knew her sister had resented the loss of privacy, resented sharing the space.

So Jessica Ann's room had become her mother's fantasy childhood bedroom. The furnishings—the nightstand, four-poster, desk, bookcase, bureau, and little corner play table where more stuffed animals dwelled—were white, the walls so light a shade of pink you could mistake them for white, too. A floral picture in color-coordinating pastels hung over the girl's bed, a lovely picture but hardly one that would be the choice of any child. Even her collection of stuffed toys had been turned into just that: a collection, a decorative touch for the perfect bed in the perfect bedroom of the perfect child.

Just about the only thing in the room that said "kid" was the one item Jessica Ann herself had picked out: the I ♥ DADDY frame with its colorful red and yellow and green lettering, in which resided a blown-up snapshot of her rugged-looking, bearded outdoorsman daddy on his boat, displaying a fish he'd caught.

"You know, it's all right to cry, Jessy."

The girl made a little shrugging gesture with her face. She was a pretty little thing, so much like her mother but with just enough baby fat to make apple cheeks out of the strong underlying cheekbones; same china-blue eyes; same perfect, slightly upturned nose; same strong yet delicate chin in the same heart-shaped face. The child's long hair, tucked back in a bun, was the sun-golden color of her mommy's cheerleading days.

"I don't exactly *feel* like crying, Aunt Beth."

Beth raised an eyebrow. "Maybe not. But . . . if you do, there's nothing wrong with it. In fact, it's good for you. Gets it out."

The child frowned, just a little. "I liked Mr. Sterling, and I'm sorry he died . . . but I don't know if I feel as sad about it as I should."

That gave Beth a chill, but just the same, she patted the girl's arm. "That's okay, too."

"Do you think Mommy's sad? I mean, *really* sad?"

"I . . . I think so. I think she is, dear. In her way."

The child glanced over at her daddy's picture. "Aunt Beth . . . do you remember how Mr. Sterling wanted me to call him 'Daddy'?"

"Well, sure, hon. What about it?"

She swallowed and the words came out haltingly. "I . . . I told him I didn't want to call him that. And I'm afraid it might've hurt his feelings . . . and now he's dead and . . ."

And suddenly there *were* tears, and Beth gathered the child in her arms; the little girl was sobbing, but trying not to.

"Let it out," Beth said, patting her, soothing her, "let it out, Jess."

After a while, the child eased out of her aunt's arms and plucked some tissues from the pale pink box on her nightstand, gathering her dignity. "But now . . . now I can't *ever* explain it to him."

"What do you mean, Jess?"

"It's just that . . ." And the child looked longingly at her daddy's picture, and touched the top of the frame, gently, barely, with her tiny perfect hand. ". . . I still call my *real* daddy 'Daddy,' when I talk to him at night."

"I'm sure Mr. Sterling understood, dear."

But Jessica Ann seemed not to hear her aunt's words; her gaze was fixed upon the photo of her father. "I was only six when he drowned in that accident . . ." Then she looked at Beth to make her point. ". . . but I remember him real good."

Beth scooched closer to Jessica Ann, patted her leg. "Sure you do, hon."

"I was mad at Mommy . . . for marrying Mr. Sterling."

"That's only natural."

"Do you think Mommy loved Mr. Sterling?"

"Well, certainly, dear—"

"Do you think she loved Daddy?"

"Of course. But, Jessy . . ." Beth searched for the words. "Your mother . . . she's kind of a . . . *special* person."

"I know," Jessica Ann said with a matter-of-fact little nod. A resigned nod. "She's very smart. And pretty."

Beth nodded back, but kept her voice positive. "She has wonderful qualities."

"She does everything for me."

"She does a lot for you. But . . . she doesn't always . . . *feel* things like maybe she should."

Jessica Ann winced in puzzlement. "What do you mean, Aunt Beth?"

Beth sighed. "It's hard to explain. She was pampered a lot—there were four of us, you know, but she was the first, and the favorite. Your grandfather, rest his soul, gave her everything." She didn't realize her voice, her smile, had turned wry, even bitter, as she said, "And why not? She was so pretty, so perfect. . . ."

"She always got her way, didn't she?"

Beth looked at her niece, mildly surprised. "How did you know that?"

Jessica Ann shrugged, and swallowed; the little gulp was as eloquent as the words that followed: " 'Cause she still does."

The girl settled back on the bed and drew her favorite stuffed animal—her teddy bear—close to her.

"Jessy," Beth began, carefully, tentatively. "I . . . I always kind of looked after your mother . . . protected her."

That drew another puzzled expression from the child. "What do you mean, Aunt Beth?"

How could she explain that sometimes the child's mother did thoughtless, even cruel things, and that somehow Beth had always known her sister couldn't help herself? That Beth had spent grade school, junior high, and even high school frequently covering up for her sister, explaining, rationalizing, and justifying her sister's behavior to other kids at school?

"It's just . . . as you grow older, Jessy, try to understand. Try to forgive her if she seems . . . well . . ."

"Cold?"

Beth sighed again, smiled sadly and nodded. "Just remember, in her way, she loves you *very* much—"

The door opened suddenly, banging a little against the wall, and Jessica Ann's mother was standing there, looking down at them. She looked like a stark emissary of death in her black dress; but a lovely one.

"Am I interrupting?" she asked with a tiny half-smile and just the hint of something critical in her tone.

"No!" Beth blurted, as if she'd been caught doing something terrible—like reading a *Goosebumps* book to Jessica Ann, for example. "No, not all. Just girl talk."

Jessica Ann's mommy tilted her head and her smile was as beautiful as it was condescending. "Isn't that sweet . . ." And now the condescension left the smile and her eyes sparkled. ". . . but not as sweet as cherry *pie*. I'm sending most of the food home with the relatives." A lilt came to her voice: "Now or never for pie and ice cream. . . ."

"*Now!*" Jessica Ann said, her apple cheeks blossoming into a smile every bit as lovely as her mommy's.

The girl scrambled off the bed and was halfway out the door when her mother snagged her gently by the shoulder and cautioned, "No running, dear, 'specially not on the stairs. More accidents happen at home, you know, than anywhere else."

Then the child was gone, and Beth sat as if waiting for a scolding.

But suddenly her sister's expression turned warm. "Can't I interest you in a slice of pie, too, Beth? And, say, wouldn't a cup of coffee go good with that, about now?"

"Sure would," she said with a smile, adding mentally, *after this long day*.

"Make some, would you? We're fresh out."

And her sister exited the bedroom. Beth sighed, patted the pointy-headed clown on its head, then trudged out of the bedroom to do her sisterly duty.

Chapter Three

March's position as chief of detectives with the Ferndale P.D. was a descriptive designation only; his actual rank was lieutenant, which reflected the grade he'd brought with him from the Chicago department, where he'd put in twenty years, mostly on the homicide detail.

He could usually be found behind a woodgrain-topped steel desk in his small office, craving a smoke, or leaning against a wall catching one, out in the little plaza area in front of the Public Safety Building. The burnt-brick multilevel modern complex, which the cops shared with the fire department, had been built ten years ago, the same year he'd taken a scenic day trip to this quiet little community of 25,000 souls to interview for the police chief opening.

March hadn't gotten the job, but a month later received a call back with an offer of a new position, a position the department wanted to create especially for him.

Ferndale sat on the banks of the Mississippi River, on the Iowa/Illinois border, on rolling land that divided much of the community into three sections: West Hill, which had been the city's Nob Hill at one time, though many of the once majestic mansions were getting long-in-the-tooth and downright rundown, now; East Hill, a residential/commercial mix with the usual shopping mall and fast food corridor on the outskirts; and Downtown, which included a quaintly charming, touristy "historic" shopping district that was making a comeback (thanks in part to the flock of antique stores that had sprung up).

But Downtown also had a less touristy attraction: a small-town version of an inner city. A large Hispanic population, whose presence dated to the days of tomato-picking migrant workers at the local Heinz plant, had never quite integrated into a community that March had come to see as sharply divided between blue- and white-collar workers, or as his sarcastic friend Detective Anderson put it, "Trailer trash and the filthy rich—you know . . . Democrats and Republicans."

The little river city *was* relatively prosperous, with a surprising number of thriving industries, including several Fortune 500 companies—with office furniture manufacturing, grain processing, tire retreading, and two chemical plants, Ferndale was a little New Jersey in the midst of Grant Wood country.

Unfortunately, Ferndale had other similarities with the east coast: drug dealing and gang activity had started to thrive here as well, about ten years ago, which was why he'd been offered the chief of detectives position. Seemed his big-city expertise was worth a salary one-third again what he made in Chicago, which, factored in with the lower cost of living in Ferndale, made the job offer downright seductive.

So was the town itself. The few blocks of gang-graffitied "inner city" couldn't diminish the charm of sleepy tree-shaded streets, turn-of-the-century Victorian homes, spacious and tasteful housing developments, a clean quiet business district, and breathtaking Mississippi River vistas from bluffs where you could view riverboats moving through the lock and dam to the quaint accompaniment of a calliope.

Not to mention no traffic jams (you could get anywhere in under ten minutes), no long waits in line at the bank or the movies . . . the good things in life went slower here, the annoying things moved faster.

The Ferndale P.D.'s other four detectives, who shared a single, bullpen-style office at the end of the hall, worked largely independently of him. His "chief of detectives" status did not require him to make their assignments, though he could pull any of them in for help on anything when he needed them.

His role was to consult with the chief on the gang problem, and to head up any major criminal investigations—usually, he defined the latter, which meant he could cherry-pick his cases. It was the dream job for any police detective.

Nonetheless, he was considering quitting.

March was a small dark man whose quietly brooding manner made him seem larger. Though approaching sixty, he had not a solitary gray hair amid a full head of widow's-peaked black; this, with his God-given tan, added up to a mournful, American Indian aspect. He wore rumpled sportshirts of dubious design—all year 'round, he brought a taste of Hawaii to Ferndale—and rumpled trousers, often denims, and on rare occasions, a rumpled sportcoat, and very occasionally a thin rumpled tie as colorless as his sportshirts were garish. His face—the strong, regular features of which had, in his youth, caused him to be called handsome—was as rumpled as his clothing, having acquired "character," the reward of a long investment in smoking and drinking, lending him the mug of a particularly good-looking bulldog.

On this unseasonably warm December afternoon, wearing only a frayed gray patched-elbow sportcoat that had been purchased in some other decade, March leaned against a wall in the Public Safety Building plaza and lighted up a Camel, as he contemplated ending his career.

Anderson, husky, fortyish, with unkempt brown hair, a ruddy complexion, and a boyish countenance, strolled up from the nearby parking lot with his partner, Coderoni, who went on in while Anderson fished a pack of Marlboros out of an overcoat pocket and joined March in a smoke.

"You still work here?" Anderson asked good-naturedly, waving out his match, the cigarette already bobbling in the sarcastic mouth. "What's a guy with your dough doing bustin' his hump in a hick town like this?"

Anderson had asked this question, in one form or another, dozens of times in the past six months.

"Glutton for punishment," March said. "Besides, it isn't my dough."

"Better yet, it's your wife's dough. Even sweeter, it's your wife's dead *husband's* dough. You know, I hear Cooney still claims he's innocent. Says you framed him."

March let out some smoke. "Absolutely I framed him. Know how I managed that?"

"Pray tell."

March patted himself on the chest. "Ventriloquism. When Cooney said all that incriminating shit in front of that lowlife hit man we wired—that was *me* talking."

"Is there no end to your talents?" Anderson said, shaking his head, laughing. Then he said, "Seriously, lieutenant, much as I'd hate to see you go, I gotta tell you, I wouldn't put in two seconds on this job if I had your wife's dough in the bank."

"That's because you lack dedication."

"You got that right. I also lack motivation, capitalization, and self-realization—although I do have constipation."

March laughed, which made Anderson smile; cracking March's poker face was the point of all the needling, after all, and it meant the younger detective had scored a point in their ongoing game.

"You know, March, you don't look like the kind of guy who even *knows* a Debbie. Let alone a rich one. Let alone be *married* to one."

"Buy a Lotto ticket, why don't you, Anderson? Maybe *you'll* get lucky."

Anderson smirked good-naturedly. "I hear you two crazy kids are takin' a full week after Christmas."

March nodded.

"Goin' anyplace special?"

"Cruise," March said with a shrug. "One of those Caribbean deals."

"Wish *I* could crack a big case," Anderson said, tossing his half-spent cigarette sizzling into a pile of snow, "and win a fair freakin' maiden."

"You'd miss me if I chucked it all," March said.

"You know," Anderson said, and grunted a laugh, "I would at that."

And the detective headed inside while March finished his Camel.

One night a little over a year ago, the CEO of a locally based, major Midwestern grocery chain had been murdered at his estate, despite high walls, guard dogs, and a sophisticated alarm system. It looked like a home invasion gone awry to the state cops, and only March had paid attention to the murdered man's wife when she insisted a disgruntled former partner of her husband's had to be behind the killing. Knowing inside information must have been supplied to skirt the heavy-duty security system, March searched for and found a leak on the household staff, which led to a local hardcase with a history of armed robbery, who had done the job—for hire. Wired by March, the lowlife met with his employer demanding more dough, getting what amounted to a confession on tape. The employer, of course, was the disgruntled partner, as the wife had predicted.

During the investigation, March and the widow had spent a lot of time together, in their common cause; and this was how a cop from Chicago had met a Debbie in Ferndale. A very wealthy Debbie, at that.

Blond, forty-eight (fifteen years younger than her late husband), Debbie was funny and smart and interested in March and his work. Or at least she had been at first—in recent weeks, she'd begun to muse about how nice it would be when he retired and they could travel and relax and just have fun together. March, who'd been married once before, had a grown son and daughter; Debbie was childless.

And her musing was starting to make sense to March. The gang problem was getting nasty—there had been three drive-by shootings in as many months, nothing by big city standards, an outrage in Ferndale. Gangbangers from Chicago were setting up crystal meth factories both in town and in country farmhouses, and it occurred to March that he had not come to sleepy Ferndale to die gut-shot in a drug raid.

Even in the most idyllic setting, even in the most benign of environments, violence dwelled.

"Lieutenant March?"

The sonorous female voice snapped him from his thoughts.

"Yes?"

She was slender and quite pretty, particularly the big brown long-lashed eyes and the fashion-model cheekbones; but her long brown hair was pinned back and she wore no makeup, and her blue thermal jacket and gloves gave her an almost dowdy, even nerdy appearance.

"We spoke on the phone," she said, sounding apologetic, and gave him her name, making a question of it. "We had an appointment? Afraid I'm a little early."

"Of course!" he said, dropping his smoked-to-the-butt cigarette to the pavement, grinding it out. "Thank you for stopping by, Beth . . . you don't mind if I call you Beth, do you? I'd like to keep this friendly."

Her brow furrowed, and impatience colored her polite manner. "What's this about, Lieutenant? I mean, I'd like to help, I like to think of myself as a good citizen, but why couldn't you tell me more when you called?"

He'd been evasive on the phone, because he knew

if he'd been direct, she might not have cooperated.

"Why don't we talk in my office," he said, and took her gently by the arm of her overstuffed jacket and walked her inside, past the dark-paneled reception area, around the corner by the dispatcher's window and down the hall.

"Can I get you some coffee, Beth?"

Their footsteps on the tile floor echoed off the cement-block walls.

"No, thank you, Lieutenant. Can we make this quick? I'm helping my sister with dinner tonight."

"You and your sister are close, I take it?"

"Why, is that unusual?"

"Not at all. Right in here, Beth. Please sit down."

When his office door was shut and she was seated across from him, still in her thermal jacket, her expression a mix of bewilderment and worry, he said, "Mrs. Sterling is actually your *half*-sister, isn't that right?"

"Yes."

He tapped his pencil on the several manila file folders stacked before him. "Is she doing all right?"

She looked at him curiously. "In what sense, Lieutenant?"

"Well, losing her husband like that. Had to be a shock. Always is."

She shifted in the metal chair. "My sister has a lot of inner strength, Lieutenant. But I've been staying there, at the house on Rockwell Road . . . with her and Jessica Ann, just to help out."

"Jessica Ann. That's the little girl—the daughter."

"Yes."

"How's *she* taking it?"

The woman unzipped her thermal jacket, but left it on; she shrugged. "We're helping her deal with it. Mr. Sterling wasn't her real father, but she was fond of him. So was I. He was a very nice man."

March nodded. He drew in a breath and then gave her what he hoped was a reassuring smile. "Beth, I'd like to stress that our conversation today isn't really official . . . that it is strictly off the record. . . ."

A corner of her mouth twitched in growing irritation. "Lieutenant, if this isn't official, why am I sitting in the police station?"

"I didn't want to bother your sister, not in her . . . time of grief. But yesterday I had a visit from Alice Jennings and Jerome Sterling . . . Mr. Sterling's daughter and son. . . ."

Her mouth twitched again. "I know who they are. Why did they visit you?"

He raised his eyebrows, set them back down again. "Frankly, they have certain . . . suspicions."

"What sort of suspicions?"

He gestured casually. "Again, this isn't official, Beth. I'm just looking for a little help in trying to ascertain whether I need to go forward on this."

"Forward on *what*?"

He began tapping on the file folders again. "I'm, uh . . . sure you've reflected on the way tragedy seems to follow your sister through life. Are you aware a classmate of hers drowned in grade school? And of course, her mother died a suicide . . ."

She sat back, blinked. "What?"

"You weren't aware of that?"

"No. No. We just . . . just knew Daddy lost his first wife under tragic circumstances."

"I see. Then, of course, your father died on a family vacation, and you lost your mother in that fire."

Her mouth tightened; so did her eyes. "Why are you going over this? I'm certainly aware that my father and mother are dead."

He nodded slowly. "And I'm sure you're aware that five years ago your sister's first husband died in a boating accident, and now of course Mr. Sterling has passed away, as well. . . ."

Her nostrils flared, her eyes, too. "Why did Alice and Jerome come to see you? What did they say? Did they accuse my sister of something?"

"No. Not directly. They did suggest that their father's death was something the police should look into."

"He died of a heart attack. He'd suffered from heart disease for many, many years. Lieutenant, I don't really think this is appropriate—"

He locked her eyes with his. "Jerome Sterling suggested your sister may have substituted placebos for Mr. Sterling's heart medication."

She glanced away, shaking her head. "My sister and her husband were devoted to each other. Why on earth would she do that?"

"According to Alice and Jerome, their father had discussed with them his intention to set up trust funds for his grandchildren—he had nine of them, you know—Alice is the mother of three children, and there are another six by his three other children, from his first marriage. This would seriously have depleted Phillip Sterling's net worth."

Now her tone was defensive. "If this is true, what makes you think my sister even knew of it?"

He locked her eyes again. "Mr. Sterling was about to retire . . . because of his age, and because of his health. He was about to sell his interest in his insurance agency. He was putting his 'house' in order. These kinds of decisions, involving community property, are difficult, even illegal, to conceal from a spouse. It's extremely likely your sister knew, Beth."

Her frown was edging into a sneer. "If you suspect Mr. Sterling died as a result of . . . what do you people call it? Foul play? Then why aren't you *officially* investigating? Why aren't you talking to my sister?"

"I'm not talking to your sister because I don't want to alarm or disturb her at a sensitive time like this. But I have to follow up on the concerns Mr. Sterling's grown children raised in this office."

"Why talk to *me* about it?"

"You're rather recently divorced, aren't you, Beth?"

Her eyes widened. "Y-yes. What does that have to—"

"You charged your husband with physical abuse, eight months ago. He spent the night in jail, and you dropped charges."

She swallowed. "That's correct."

"Several months later your husband . . . ex-husband . . . had a bad fall in your house."

"He got drunk and fell down the stairs, yes."

"He called 911 and reported not only his fall, but the presence of an intruder in the house."

Her expression mingled confusion and irritation. "Yes. So . . . ?"

"Detective Anderson interviewed your husband at the hospital. Your husband, Robert, said your sister pushed him."

Her eyes widened again, then narrowed. "That's the first I heard of any such thing."

"That's because he withdrew the accusation almost immediately." He lifted one of the file folders. "But it's in Anderson's notes, just the same."

"What are you getting at?"

He shrugged again. "It's just that I continue to be fascinated by the way tragedy follows your sister around. Remember that character in *Li'l Abner* with the dark cloud hovering over him?"

"No."

"Beth . . ."

"What?"

". . . Do you think your sister's capable of . . . pushing your husband down the stairs?"

She stood and leaned a hand against his desk and her words were tightly indignant. "And murdering her husband? You're out of line, Lieutenant. Way out of line. My sister is a good person. A wonderful person. Do you have any idea of how active she's been in this community, with the United Way, with her church, with . . . but of course you are. That's part of why you're afraid to embarrass yourself by questioning her. You're more comfortable pushing the little sister around, some poor meek little pre-school teacher you can intimidate and manipulate with your 'friendly' questioning."

She turned and moved quickly to the door.

He caught her there with: "Beth!"

She turned and gave him a slow burn, but waited to hear what he had to say.

"Do me one favor," March said. "Don't mention our conversation to your sister."

She gave out a single humorless laugh. "I'll do you that favor. With her connections, you wouldn't want to make an enemy of her."

And she was gone.

March smiled to himself, surprised by the spine the "little sister" had shown. There was a reservoir of strength inside that "meek" woman.

He rubbed his forehead, sending his fingers up through his hair, scratching his scalp, in a mannerism that accompanied his most intense thinking. Then he said, "Hunh," to nobody, and went out and down the hall into the bullpen area, to get himself a cup of coffee.

Back at his desk, sipping his coffee, he picked up the phone receiver and pushed buttons, reading the number off a Post-it on one of the manila file folders. When he got Consolidated Life on the phone, he asked for Patterson, the investigating agent in charge.

"I don't think there's much to go on, on this end," March said. "I mean, we've got an autopsy that Mrs. Sterling requested herself, and an official finding of heart failure as cause of death. There's just nothing to justify any sort of homicide investigation."

"No decision's been made on this end yet, either," Patterson said. "If we determine further fact finding's in order, we'll keep you in the loop."

"You damn well better," March said. "If we do have a black-widow murder here, it's mine. Understood?"

"No problem," Patterson said.

Hanging up, March felt the familiar tingle. Even though this was probably a false alarm, he relished the thought of a juicy murder case.

And he didn't think about quitting his job for the rest of the day.

Chapter Four

It was on the second Thursday in April at McKinley Elementary School, the very afternoon she received her excellent Basic Skills test results, which had made the child happy because she knew it would make her mother happy, that Jessica Ann sensed the first storm warning.

During the afternoon study period, Mrs. Withers had asked Jessica Ann to step out in the hall. A murmur passed across the fifth-grade classroom, because this procedure invariably signaled a scolding—praise was administered by calling a student up to the desk for whispered words of commendation—and Jessica Ann, the best student in class, the best-behaved student in school, was an unlikely recipient of such a summons.

Confused, even alarmed, the child rose from her

desk—she sat in front, near the window, looking out on the playground—and smoothed her navy dress over her white leggings, adjusted the red bow at her neck, ill at ease as she walked across the front line of the still murmuring classroom.

Mrs. Withers waited at the door for Jessica Ann to step into the hall, then closed it behind them.

The teacher, fiftyish, brown cap of curls just beginning to gray, her stout frame clad in a powder-blue pantsuit, always made an imposing figure; now she seemed to loom over the petite child. But as Jessica Ann gazed up at this tall thick-trunked tree of a woman, she was relieved to see the sometimes stern countenance of Mrs. Withers cast in a sympathetic smile.

"I didn't mean to embarrass you, Jessica Ann," Mrs. Withers said, "but we couldn't talk in front of the class, and if I were to ask you to stay after, you'd miss your bus."

Jessica Ann couldn't think of a response to this, so she just smiled timidly.

"I'm very proud of you, Jessica Ann. You scored in the ninety-ninth percentile in every grouping on your Basic Skills . . . the highest ranking possible, and certainly the highest ranking in class."

"Thank you, ma'am."

The smile on Mrs. Withers's face seemed to fade; something was troubling the woman.

"Let's sit and talk for just a few seconds," Mrs. Withers suggested, and pulled over two desk-chairs used by the hall monitors. She gestured for Jessica

Ann to sit, and the child did, and Mrs. Withers pulled the chair around so that when she sat, she was facing Jessica Ann, which she did with folded hands and a solemn expression, though it was hard for the big lady to squeeze into the little chair.

"I'm going to be announcing soon," Mrs. Withers said, "who will receive the Outstanding Student of the Year award." She sighed and looked away, rolling her eyes in an expression of exasperation all of her students were well familiar with. "Frankly, if I had my way, I'm not certain I wouldn't do away with the award altogether."

This seemed a puzzling remark, and Jessica Ann said, "Why, Mrs. Withers?"

Now here was the familiar stern look. "Because I'm not at all convinced such competition is a positive thing for you children. Making one child feel good at the expense of the rest of the class seems to me a poor trade."

Jessica Ann said nothing, but something in her downcast expression prompted Mrs. Withers to smile and pat her on the arm. "Not that you should feel bad about winning an award like that. You won how many times in the past?"

"Three."

"Second, third and fourth grades—Outstanding Student of the Year, every time. You should be proud. I'm sure your mother is."

"Yes, ma'am."

Mrs. Withers's smile seemed rather forced now. "But then, of course, you realize no one can win *every* year. For example, you didn't win in the first grade, did you?"

"I didn't go to McKinley in the first grade, ma'am. We didn't have the award at my other school."

"I see." Mrs. Withers sighed. "At any rate, I wanted you to know how highly I regard you and your scholastic achievements."

"Thank you, ma'am."

The teacher frowned, but it wasn't an angry frown; her dark blue eyes were kind. "But Jessica Ann, I want you to be prepared. I don't want you to be disappointed . . . and while you're certainly among the top students in class, arguably the finest in this or any class at McKinley . . . you will not be receiving the award this year."

"Oh. Well . . . that's all right."

Mrs. Withers was shaking her head slowly, side to side. "I know it must mean a lot to you, Jessica Ann . . ."

Actually, it didn't. Sure, it was nice winning awards, and the gold plaques looked cool on her bedroom wall; but she knew very well that a good number of her classmates resented her for her consistently high marks; nobody likes a smart kid, nobody likes a kid who wrecks the grading curve.

"That's okay, Mrs. Withers. It's really not that important . . . to me."

The teacher's brow furrowed with concern. "You say that as if it's important to . . . someone else?"

"I . . . I just don't know what my mommy's going to say."

"I see," Mrs. Withers said, nodding. "Will she be mad at you?"

"I'm not sure. I've never had a bad grade before. . . ."

"This isn't a bad grade, Jessica Ann. Do you want me to talk to her about it?"

"No! I mean . . . it won't be necessary."

Mrs. Withers leaned forward. "I'll tell you a secret, if you promise not to repeat it to any of your classmates."

"Sure."

She tapped gently with a finger on the child's arm. "If I were going strictly by grades, test results, and classroom behavior, you would win the award. Hands down."

"Oh. Well, then . . . nothing."

Mrs. Withers drew back, folding her arms, half-smiling. "Then why aren't *you* receiving the award? Because, Jessica Ann, I also take into consideration other factors, such as if a student has improved, if a student has made concerted efforts that have brought him or her up to honor roll level. Particularly a student who hasn't enjoyed some of the advantages other students might have."

"It's okay, Mrs. Withers. Really."

Mrs. Withers raised her chin. "I think you have a right to know the student's name I've selected—it's Eduardo Melindez. He's made remarkable strides this year, and I hope this award will encourage him to continue bettering himself."

Jessica Ann smiled and nodded.

This response pleased Mrs. Withers. "Do you agree with me that Eduardo is a good choice?"

She shrugged. "Sure. He has grades almost as good as mine."

"We have a substantial Hispanic community in Ferndale, Jessica Ann, and our school system hasn't always treated them fairly. I'm trying, in my small way, to compensate for certain injustices."

"That's fine. Really, I don't mind. Eduardo's nice."

Mrs. Withers studied the child for what seemed an eternity to the girl but was really a few seconds. "Jessica Ann, may I ask you a personal question?"

"Okay."

"Who's your best friend?"

She almost reflexively said, *You are, Mommy*, but caught herself. "I have lots of friends."

"Do you? Sometimes, being an outstanding student isn't always an advantage when it comes to your peers. Other children, I mean."

Jessica Ann shrugged again. "I get along with everybody."

"I know. I've observed that. . . . You know, Jessica Ann, you really do dress beautifully. You're a beautifully groomed young lady."

"Thank you."

Mrs. Withers had a distant expression for a moment. "You remind me of a day when children dressed for school as if they were going to church. . . . Of course, now they don't even dress very well for church. Does your mother help you pick out your things?"

"N-no."

Mrs. Withers seemed doubtful. "She doesn't?"

"She doesn't help me. She does it herself. Sometimes I come along. . . ."

"I see. I notice you never wear slacks or jeans to school, like most of the other girls."

"Sometimes Mommy lets me wear culottes."

"Is that why you're never really very active at recess? Why you so often just stay inside and read?"

Jessica Ann nodded. "Mommy says nice clothes only stay that way if you take care of them."

Mrs. Withers shook her head and smiled wide. "Well, you certainly do look like you stepped out of a bandbox."

"Pardon?"

"Nothing. Just betraying my age, dear. Are you . . . all right, with what we've discussed? About Eduardo and this year's award?"

"Yes, ma'am."

Mrs. Withers scooted the little desk-chair back and stood. "Then let's go back in, shall we?"

That evening, Aunt Beth was over for supper, in fact she cooked the supper, spaghetti with homemade sauce, a family favorite. It was a recipe that originated with Mommy and Aunt Beth's father—Jessica Ann's late grandfather, who she'd never known—and usually Mommy fussed over how good it was, much to Aunt Beth's pleasure; but tonight Mommy was morose and moody.

Which was really frustrating, because Jessica Ann's mind was alive with what Mrs. Withers had told her. She knew her mother would be upset about the award, possibly even angry, but holding this inside was torture. Still, with her mother in this dark state of mind, now was hardly the time to spring disappointing news.

After a largely silent, gloomy, but delicious supper, Jessica Ann went up to her room and sat at her little desk, doing her homework. Her three Outstanding Student awards—wooden plaques with gold face-plates and bold black lettering—OUTSTANDING STUDENT OF THE YEAR, JESSICA ANN STERLING, MCKINLEY SCHOOL—were on the wall in front of her, SECOND GRADE, THIRD GRADE, FOURTH GRADE, stairstepping down. Their presence tormented the child until she felt as though she might burst; she needed at once to unburden herself *and* get her mother's negative reaction out of the way.

She moved to the bed, to get away from the nagging award plaques, and finished her math and geography—the only homework she had tonight—and then looked at her fisherman father in the I ♥ DADDY frame, as if for advice. His friendly smile seemed to encourage her to go talk to Mommy.

She padded out into the darkened hall, but voices from the living room rose up the open stairwell, slightly echoey, but clear enough to follow.

"Do you want to talk?" Aunt Beth's voice asked.

"I'm in no mood," Mommy said. "*No* mood."

"Might do you some good, Sis. . . ."

No response.

Then Aunt Beth's voice again: "Your appointment

with Ekhardt must not have gone well."

Jessica Ann crouched and clutched the rungs of the hallway banister that overlooked the stairwell and entryway. This was a familiar eavesdropping position for the child.

"Neal is a dear," Mommy's voice sighingly replied, "and a fine attorney—just the right touch of sleaze to really look after a girl, you know? But I'm afraid Phillip had better legal counsel than I."

"Surely you can't begrudge him leaving a portion of his estate to his children, and his grandchildren—"

"They're vultures," Mommy snapped. "The only ones who even bothered to come to the funeral were fat Alice and dear Jerome. The three doofuses by wife number one didn't bother to make the trip, and they're all within a three-state radius; not a single precious grandchild was present. Do you know Alice and Jerome complained about me to the insurance company?"

"Complained . . . complained how?"

"How should I know? I just know I had to answer embarrassing, humiliating questions to some awful investigator over the phone."

"When was this?" Aunt Beth sounded concerned.

Mommy didn't. "I don't know. Early January."

"You never mentioned it."

"Wasn't important. They've put my claim through, and that's all I care about. That and that fate headed off Phillip before he had the chance to leave Jessica Ann and me in dire financial straits. I'm just lucky

Phillip did me the courtesy of passing away before he put those ridiculous trust funds into effect for his stupid grandchildren."

The cruelty of Mommy's words splashed Jessica Ann like cold water.

Aunt Beth sounded aghast. "Don't say that. That's terrible."

Mommy's voice carried a brittle indignation. "What's *terrible* is the way Phillip Sterling misled me. He portrayed himself as wealthy. Wealthy! That's a laugh. This house isn't even paid off. And if I'd known how much of his property and holdings were already designated for the fruit of his loins by those other two witches he married . . ."

Only Jessica Ann wasn't sure Mommy said "witches."

". . . I would never have married that charlatan in the first place."

Shock put a tremor in Aunt Beth's voice. "You . . . you don't mean that."

"No." Mommy's voice shifted. It seemed to modulate into something more reasonable, as if she too knew she'd gone too far. "No . . . I suppose I don't. I loved Phillip. He was good to us. Please, forget what I said, Beth. I shouldn't have let you talk me into that second glass of wine after dinner. You know I detest alcohol. I detest anything that makes me lose control of my faculties."

"Why don't I go," Aunt Beth said. "You can get to bed early. You obviously had a pretty rough session today with those lawyers. . . ."

Footsteps echoed below as the two sisters moved into the entryway.

"I'm fine, Beth. You're a dear. And I didn't even compliment you on your famous spaghetti! Daddy couldn't have done a better job himself."

From her perch between the rungs of the railing, Jessica Ann watched as Mommy guided her sister to the door, helping her into her overstuffed jacket, allowing Aunt Beth to kiss her on the cheek. Then Mommy gave Aunt Beth a radiant smile, which brightened Beth's expression before Mommy closed the door and the smile disappeared.

Jessica Ann didn't know if Mommy had sensed her watching or not; just as Mommy seemed about to glance upward, Jessica Ann pulled back from her eavesdropping perch and scampered back into her bedroom. The child flopped back onto her bed and began rechecking her math problems.

Mommy knocked, then cracked open the door and peeked in, remaining poised in the doorway; she was still in the black jacket and white dress she'd worn to the lawyers, and though this was near the end of a long day, including two glasses of wine, she looked immaculate, every platinum hair in place.

"Ah," she said, "you're doing your homework. Good girl."

"Did Aunt Beth leave, Mommy?"

Still in the doorway, Mommy nodded. "She has to work tomorrow."

"Supper was good."

"Yes. Jessica Ann, you were very quiet at dinner."

The child was always quiet at dinner, but Mommy had excellent instincts about her daughter's moods. Jessica Ann had never learned to hide her feelings sufficiently to escape her mother's inquiries.

"You seemed tired," Jessica Ann said, sitting up. "I just didn't want to bother you."

Mommy moved to the bed, moved a math book out of the way, and sat on the edge, keeping a certain distance between her and the girl. "Didn't you forget to tell me something?"

"What, Mommy?"

"You got your Basic Skills results back today, didn't you?"

"Yes. How did you—"

"Your principal called to congratulate me. You had the highest results in your grade, didn't you?"

"Yes."

Mommy's smile was tight as she patted the girl, once, on the shoulder. "Jessica Ann, you mustn't be shy about your accomplishments. Something this important, and you didn't even tell me. . . ."

"I'm sorry, Mommy."

Mommy's smile softened as she shook her head. "You mustn't feel ashamed of being superior to others. It's a blessing, dear. A gift. When you say your prayers tonight, I want you to send God a great big thank-you note for making you so intelligent."

"I will, Mommy. Mommy . . . there's something else. . . ."

Mommy's eyebrows lifted, her lovely china-blue eyes filled with patient interest. "What, dear?"

"I talked to Mrs. Withers today. She wanted to talk to me, special."

"I should hope she would, after what you accomplished."

"It's not that. She wanted to tell me that even though I'm a very good student, I . . . I'm not going to get the Outstanding Student Award this year."

Mommy's eyes narrowed and hardened; at the outside corner of her left eye, a slight tic twitched. She fired her words like bullets: "What? Why not?"

Jessica Ann shrugged. "She's . . . she's giving it to another student, that's all. She said I was the best student, but that there were other considerations."

"What sort of 'considerations'?"

"Some kids don't have the advantages that I have."

"Do you know who the winner is?"

"Yes."

"Who is she? Or it a he?"

"It's a he, Mommy. His name is Eduardo Melindez."

Mommy's faint smile wasn't really a smile at all. "Really. How multicultural of your teacher. How politically, insufferably correct. Does the boy speak English?"

"*Of course* he speaks English, Mommy."

"That's nice. Dear, the award isn't given until the PTA meeting next month. Perhaps there's still time to do something about this."

Jessica Ann lurched forward, even as something awful leapt in her breast. "I don't want you to do anything about it, Mommy—"

"Dear, I won't allow my little girl to be treated unfairly." She stood, tucking her hands behind her. "Who's your best friend?"

Jessica Ann, sitting on the bed, mimicked the gesture. "You are, Mommy."

Mommy put a hand on her heart and looked down at her daughter with a lovely smile. "Who loves you more than anything on God's green earth?"

Jessica Ann covered her heart. "You do, Mommy."

"Good." Mommy stood. "Lights out at nine, dear. Brush your teeth first!"

"Yes, Mommy."

Then Mommy, glancing past Jessica Ann with a frown, moved around the bed, going to her daughter's little desk. Leaning forward, Mommy adjusted each of the Outstanding Student plaques, making sure every one was hanging perfectly straight, then surveyed her work with a keen eye and nodded in self-satisfaction before leaving her daughter's room.

Chapter Five

Beth's reaction to the entry of Mark Jeffries into her sister's life induced contradictory impulses within her that were all too typical in the relationship between the two sisters. She was at once happy for her sister's good romantic fortune, and—particularly during tossing-turning nights, before giving in and rising to take her sleep medication—deeply, bitterly envious.

They had met Mark on the same evening in February, at a country club affair. Beth, of course, was not a member, but the wife of Phillip Sterling certainly was, who—after over a month of dutiful mourning—was anxious to get out into the world once again. Members could bring nonmember guests, and since it would be grossly improper for the recently widowed Mrs. Sterling to attend with a date, Beth had accepted her sister's invitation to come along and keep her company.

It was a dinner dance, with a Valentine's Day sweetheart theme that made Beth uncomfortable; the presence of the two sisters, alone at a side table, seemed absurd in these circumstances. In her navy wool-crepe jacket and white silk slacks, Beth felt like the substitute male next to her flamboyantly feminine sister, whose shocking pink dress with its lacy, tiered top and cascading chiffon skirt was a bold announcement of her withdrawal from widow's weeds. Beth had felt so chic at home, preening in front of her mirror; but in her stunning sister's shapely reflection, she saw herself boyishly dowdy.

Beth was the first to spot him. Elegant in a gray Armani suit with blue-and-gray deco tie, the slender six-footer with the immaculately trimmed salt-and-pepper beard and tropical tan stood sipping a Manhattan, his Rolex catching the light and winking at her, as he chatted with Ralph and Sarah Beckey out on the dance floor, where conversational clusters had formed. Beth figured him to be about thirty-five, and he had a rich baritone laugh that rose over the cocktail-party chatter, accompanied by a dazzling smile that was the male equivalent of her sister's, only with warmth stirred in.

"Do you know who that is?" Beth asked her sister.

"No. . . ." And as she studied him carefully, a smile began to tickle her valentine-red lips. ". . . but I think I'd *like* to."

"He must be here on business. He just doesn't look like somebody from Ferndale."

"Not unless they're hiring at Hanley's again," she said, referring to a local architectural consulting firm. The china-blue eyes had taken on an acquisitive glaze Beth knew all too well. "My guess is the east coast. . . ."

Then, in a friendly manner that meant she wanted something, Beth's sister leaned toward the next table and asked the wife of the First National Bank's CEO if she knew who the handsome newcomer was.

"That's Mark Jeffries," the banker's wife said, seated momentarily alone while her husband got her another refill on her martini. She was a darkly attractive, Liz Taylor–ish woman of about fifty-five. "Came to town last month from New York—he's moving his business here, and I hear he's pretty well off."

"Is he banking at First National?"

"I believe so."

"Then you'd be in a position to know."

"He wouldn't have to have a dime to put his Italian loafers under my bed. . . . I didn't say that." She sighed dreamily. "Looks like he stepped off a *GQ* cover, doesn't he?"

"Breath of fresh air after our farm-grown variety of male," she said.

"I'm surprised you haven't met him already," the banker's wife continued, "considering he's here as Ralph's guest."

Jovial, heavy-set, balding Ralph Beckey had been Mr. Sterling's late partner.

"Ralph is sponsoring Mark for club membership," the banker's wife added.

Ferndale Golf and Country Club was a venerable local institution, but this facility was brand spanking new, a glittering modern multimillion-dollar complex on the edge of the city, a gift to themselves by a handful of Ferndale's wealthiest families. The club had an outdoor Olympic-size pool, a stable of riding horses, and a host of tennis courts. Its dining room looked out on one of the best (and most beautifully landscaped and forest-encircled) eighteen-hole golf courses in the Midwest. If Mark Jeffries's urbane demeanor set him immediately apart, the well-to-do of this Midwestern community were not strangers to designer dress, and there were enough diamonds and other precious jewels in the club dining room tonight to open a Ferndale branch of Tiffany's. Beth could not have felt more out of place here if she'd been wearing clown shoes.

She knew her sister was bursting to make contact with Mark Jeffries, but—like any good predator—was biding her time. The widow in pink made no effort to move within the borders of the Beckeys' conversational circle, but did sashay along their periphery when the sisters were among the first to go the salad bar.

No question about it—Mark Jeffries had noticed the stunning blonde in lace and chiffon. He'd noticed Beth, too—he'd smiled at her, as she and her sister moved past with their salad plates in hand.

But when the Beckeys began table-hopping after supper, just as the little three-piece jazz-band combo began playing "The Good Life," Beth could sense her sister's irritation begin to bubble into that familiar dry-ice rage.

"That lardbucket Ralph Beckey is snubbing me," she said, barely touching her cheesecake, her unblinking blue eyes shooting death rays. "He still hasn't gotten over my insisting on that audit."

"What audit?" Beth asked, pushing aside the rest of her carrot cake.

Her sister shrugged. "Phillip's net worth just didn't ring true to me. I had the legal right to have the business audited by an outside accounting firm, and I did."

"Well . . . you may've had the right to do that, Sis, but you probably don't have the right to expect him to—"

But at that moment, Ralph, his wife, and their guest did make their way to the Sterling table, all smiles and good cheer—and Beth and her sister greeted them the same way.

On closer examination, Mark Jeffries's handsome features had a weathered, just slightly worn cast that gave him a certain ruggedness, but which also had Beth revising his age estimate upward, closer to forty—and the gray-blue eyes in the smiling face had a permanent tinge of melancholy.

"I understand you've been through a difficult

time," Mark said to Beth's sister, after the introductory rituals were over.

"Yes," she said. And she turned what seemed to be a gracious gaze upon Ralph Beckey. "But everyone's been so kind and understanding."

The veiled insult seemed to sail right over Ralph's bald head. He said, "You know, you lovely ladies could do me a big favor, this evening. I talked Mark here into coming tonight, and I hadn't really thought it through—I mean, this is pretty much a couples evening, and that leaves a bachelor like him hanging high and dry. If you could find it in your sweet hearts to give him a dance or two—"

"Ralph, please," Mark said, smiling but obviously embarrassed.

"I'd love to dance, Mr. Jeffries," Beth's sister said, standing, and cast that beguiling smile of hers on him. The little combo was playing "Call Me Irresponsible."

Beth had seen her sister work her magic on many a defenseless male over the years, and Mark Jeffries was no exception. He was displaying many of the classic symptoms: the dazed look in his eyes, the slackening of his mouth, the deferential way he took her hand as she led her benumbed subject onto the dance floor. . . .

But as Beth sat alone with her glass of chablis, trying to swallow her envy with the wine, watching the couple glide about the dance floor, talking, laughing, eyes locked except when cheek to cheek, she realized suddenly her sister seemed as entranced as Mark Jeffries did. Was this part of her performance? Or was a man for once touching something inside of her?

Finally the couple returned to the table, and Mark asked Beth to dance—as a courtesy, she supposed, just feeling sorry for her—and Beth smiled politely and declined.

"You two are doing just fine," Beth said.

"Don't be silly," her sister said, gathering her purse. "I'm going to the little girl's room. I'll collect him in due time."

And in a pink haze of lace and chiffon, she was off.

Mark watched her with the dazed look of a clubbed baby seal.

Beth risked a smirk. "She's asserting her ownership a little early."

He looked at Beth, shook his head as if clearing cobwebs, and a grin appeared in the well-tended nest of beard. "Your sister is a remarkable woman."

"Yes she is. You really don't have to dance with me, Mr. Jeffries."

"Mark. And I really do. I haven't known your sister very long, but I'm already getting the feeling that if she wants us to dance . . . we damn well better dance."

Beth laughed a little, and then she and Mark were gliding around the dance floor to a particularly bittersweet arrangement of "My Funny Valentine." His cologne had an outdoorsy fragrance that was perhaps too heavy, but she liked it anyway, and she liked his eyes, sensitive eyes, kind eyes, their long lashes almost feminine, though offset by thickly masculine eyebrows.

"Your sister's doing very well," he said.

"In what sense?"

"I mean . . . losing her husband . . ."

"Oh. Yes, she's nothing if not resilient."

"Are you close?"

"We . . . see a lot of each other. Rest of the family is hither and yon. I spend a lot of time with Jessica Ann."

"Jessica Ann?"

"Yes—her little girl by her first marriage."

"Ah."

"Jessica Ann is a dear. She's ten, but a very old soul."

He seemed to be reflecting on that, then suddenly he said, "Are you married, Beth?"

"Divorced."

"Any kids, yourself?"

"No."

"Why do I think you're *recently* divorced. . . ."

She shrugged. "Maybe because I am."

"So. How are *you* doing?"

"Well, I'm not as resilient as my sister, but I'm doing all right. She was very supportive about that."

"Your sister?"

"Yes. My husband was kind of a creep, tended to get kind of, you know, physical, and . . . well, my sister is good in a crisis. She can rise to most occasions."

"What do you do?"

"I work at a preschool."

"Like it?"

She nodded. "I love kids. They're pure in a way adults rarely are. Funny."

"What?"

"Just occurred to me. One of the things about my sister that I most admire . . . I can't say it's a quality I *like* exactly . . . but she's the only person I've ever known who's never changed."

"What do you mean?"

Beth shrugged. "She's been the way she is since childhood."

"And what way is that?"

"Perfect."

He laughed. "Come on now, Beth, you know what they say. . . ."

"Nobody's perfect? She comes close."

"I've only known your sister for a few minutes . . . but I get the distinct feeling a fairly selfish heart beats beneath that attractive . . . well, you know what I mean."

"Oh, she's selfish all right—but perfectly selfish."

He laughed again. "Well, I'll tell you one thing—she has a perfectly delightful sister."

Warmth rushed to her face; embarrassment? What?

"You're very sweet," she said, almost mumbling.

The song ended and, as they were walking back to the table, where her sister had not yet returned, he asked, "Is your sister a perfect mother, too?"

"Maybe a little too perfect."

"Overprotective?"

"Terribly so. Jessica Ann is awfully sheltered. . . ."

He shrugged. "In this day and age, is that such a bad thing?"

Beth had one other dance with Mark that evening, during which he told her a little bit about his mail-order business—seemed he'd gotten very successful selling audio books via a direct-mail catalogue. It had started as a part-time project (he'd been in advertising, before) and just took off. He was maintaining a small staff back east, where all the orders were taken and filled; now that he'd relocated to Ferndale, all he would do from his office in the Laurel Building was review product and prepare his next catalogue, and of course maintain daily contact with his staff in Trenton by phone and fax.

"The global village is a wonderful thing," he told Beth as they danced to "The Shadow of Your Smile."

"You mean, you listen to books all day?"

"That's part of what I do. It's the kind of business that requires a personal touch . . . I write the copy myself. Sort of like J. Crew, only books. Audio books."

"You mean like, self-help?"

"That, plus fiction, nonfiction. I'll give you one of my catalogues."

With the exception of dancing twice with Mark, and once with Ralph Beckey, Beth sat alone at the little table all that evening, getting quietly tipsy on wine, watching her sister dance with the sort of good-looking, sensitive, intelligent man Beth knew she would probably never land.

She didn't blame her sister; she envied her, but the fault lay with Beth herself. She knew that. She knew she'd never gone after nice, smart guys with good jobs—she'd never dared. Never considered herself good enough, contenting herself with blue-collar louses looking for an easy lay and a punching bag.

These, at least, had been her thoughts after an indeterminate number of glasses of wine.

In the weeks that followed, Beth watched her sister and Mark become an item in record time—though it was hard to tell just who was sweeping who off whose feet. Oddly, after that first night at the country club, Mark kept arm's length from Beth, remaining friendly but not confiding in her, or questioning her about her sister either, the way previous beaux from Chad Harrison to Phillip Sterling had.

Actually, it relieved her that Mark didn't seem to view her in that "kid sister" manner; Beth liked to think Mark was keeping his distance because he was attracted to her, that he didn't trust himself around her.

Deep down, though, she figured she was just kidding herself.

Still, Mark was a good influence on the Sterling household. He and Jessica Ann got along famously. Beth, who frequently took (and helped prepare) supper at the house on Rockwell Road, was pleasantly surprised by the rapport that quickly developed between the child and her mother's new boyfriend. Jessica Ann was quiet, even shy around most adults, but she would sit on the couch and talk to Mark and, more importantly, he would talk to her, without an ounce of condescension.

Beth tried not to eavesdrop, but the discussion she'd caught part of, tonight, was fairly typical.

"I don't really care about the award, Mark," Jessica Ann was saying.

"It seems to mean a lot to your mother."

"But I don't want her making a fuss at school. . . ."

"Do you want me to talk to her about it?"

The relief in the child's voice was heartbreaking. "Would you? Please?"

"Sure, angel. No guarantees, though. Your mommy has a mind of her own."

"*Tell* me about it."

But the most extraordinary example of Mark's influence on her sister had come that night. Mark had spent the evening watching television with Jessica Ann, her mother, and Beth—something of a rarity in and of itself, because this was not much of a TV-watching household—but Mark had rented *Beauty and the Beast*, and it made a big hit with everyone.

Now Mark was gone, and Jessica Ann was upstairs in her room, getting ready for bed; and Beth and her sister were having coffee at the table in the kitchen's large dining area.

Her sister sipped at her coffee and said, too casually, "Do you think I'm foolish?"

The question blindsided Beth. "You? Never."

She shrugged with her eyebrows. "*I* think I'm foolish. I'm rushing in. Moving too fast."

Beth leaned forward. "Mark's a wonderful guy. If you don't grab him, somebody else will."

"What will people think?" Her brow was furrowed, her eyes tight. "They must be talking already."

"That maybe it's too soon after Phillip's death for you to be seeing somebody? I don't think so."

Neither, apparently, did her sister, whose reply was, "You know, I've never been with a younger man before."

"He's not that much younger."

Her sister was shaking her head. "I'm acting like a schoolgirl. It isn't like me."

"It's good for you. I'm happy for you, Sis."

"You are, aren't you?" The china-blue eyes were quietly astounded; it was as if experiencing another person's emotions vicariously was a foreign concept to her.

"Yes," Beth said, "very happy for you."

The woman looked into her coffee cup, studying her shimmering reflection in the dark liquid. "Jessica Ann seems to accept him."

"I'll say. I think if you don't marry him, she will."

"Who said anything about marriage?"

Beth smirked, sipped her own coffee. "You're the marrying kind, Sis. You always have been."

"He has money. He could support us well."

"What does that have to do with anything?"

"I like to be practical."

Beth's tone was archly sarcastic as she said, "You mean, you wouldn't want to marry a man just because you loved him?"

But her sister's reply was flat: "That's right." Then she said, "How awful would it look if I allowed him to sleep over sometimes?"

Beth, astounded by what was already the most personal, soul-baring conversation she could remember ever having with her sister, asked, "Have you been with him yet? Has it gone that far?"

Now her sister's eyes grew cold. "That's personal, Beth. Hypothetically . . . if I were to sleep with him, could I do it here? Would people talk?"

"Would you care?"

"Yes."

Beth laughed humorlessly, sipped her coffee again, shook her head, and said, "Sis . . . there's something I don't understand about you. On the one hand, you seem to care very much about appearances."

Her sister's expression was blank as she matter-of-factly nodded her head, saying, "That's true."

"On the other hand, you frequently do whatever pleases you at a given moment, and to hell with the circumstances."

Her sister shrugged. "One has to have priorities."

Beth rolled her eyes. "I see. Sis, your priority here should be your own happiness, and Jessica Ann's. Mark would make a wonderful father for her . . . and even if you don't marry the guy, for right now, he provides your daughter a strong father figure."

She was nodding, her eyes glazed with consideration. "It's nice that he's younger. Phillip was so old, he was more like a grandfather to Jessica Ann. Do you think it sets a harmful example to Jessica Ann if he stays over?"

"Social standards have changed since we were kids, Sis. I think she'll adjust to that just fine."

Her sister's blank mask blossomed into a surprisingly warm smile. "Thank you, Beth." She reached over and patted Beth's hand, once. "Every girl should have a sister like you."

It was perhaps the nicest thing, the kindest thing, her sister had ever said to her; Beth might have gotten teary-eyed, if she hadn't been so startled.

But the gesture emboldened Beth to venture into forbidden waters.

"Sis, can I ask you something about Jessica Ann?"

Another smile, but a perfunctory one, accompanied her response: "What, dear?"

"This . . . Outstanding Student Award. She's awfully upset about it."

Her sister sipped her coffee, shrugged a tiny shrug. "As well she should be. She deserves that award."

"That's not why she's upset. She's afraid you're mad at her for not winning it. . . ."

"But she *did* win it."

"That's not what I understood. . . ."

Her sister's expression would have frozen Medusa to stone. "This is my business, Beth, and I intend to handle it *my*-self. I have a parent-teacher conference tomorrow with the woman responsible for this outrage."

"Couldn't you just let it go? Jessica Ann—"

"Is *my* concern."

And the cold calm that settled over her sister's face as she rose to carry her empty coffee cup to the sink meant that there would be no more discussion of this topic, and no more Hallmark moments, either.

Beth had to take double her usual dosage that night.

Chapter Six

McKinley Elementary, a rust-brown brick building that sat well back from quiet, residential Kindler Avenue, had been the pride of the Ferndale school system in 1961, when it was built. Now the once modern one-story square-doughnut-shaped structure was in serious need of refurbishing, with 400 students crowding its 300-student capacity, a roof requiring asbestos removal, computer age–deficient electrical and telephone wiring, inadequate handicap accessibility, and an outmoded furnace system that required an area the size of the boiler room of the *Titanic*.

The outer structure presented itself well; McKinley still looked new, and modern, particularly to residents old enough to remember the 1905 structure it had replaced, and the local taxpayers had voted down the school bond issue, last fall, that would have addressed the decay lurking behind the immaculate, attractive facade.

A long, wide walk cut straight through a tree-shaded, shrubbery-dotted, well-tended lawn to a generous half-circle loading zone, where on this quiet afternoon in early May, school buses were just starting to roll in, in anticipation of three o'clock dismissal. On its silver pole near the bicycle racks, the American flag flapped in a slight, soothing breeze. The sun was out, but it wasn't quite a sunny afternoon, not with unthreatening but quickly moving clouds casting cool blue shadows over the brick building, the cement walk, the green grass, the yellow buses.

The bell rang shrilly, and soon the students of McKinley were herded down the hall and inside the gym, whose leaky roof was a continual problem, where two teachers whose unlucky duty it was to be on bus duty today did their best to line the unruly students up for their individual buses—a hopeless, thankless task. The voices of the kids—shouts, laughter, squeals—echoed hysterically in the gym; no one really expected them to behave at the end of a long day, penned up in here waiting to go home. Certainly not the benign presence in a belted burgundy dress, wending her way amongst them: Mrs. Evans, principal of McKinley, nearing retirement, a diminutive, attractive woman with short, carefully coiffed brown hair and the kind eyes and patient smile only those whose true calling was teaching could have retained at her age.

Oddly, the only child that caught Mrs. Evans's attention was not an obnoxious misbehaving little brat, rather the quietest child in the gym, standing alone along the wall against a hanging wrestling mat, not lining up, looking as glum as she did pretty in her white lacy blouse and blue suspendered culottes: Jessica Ann Sterling.

"Why aren't you in line, dear?" Mrs. Evans asked.

"I'm waiting for my mother, Mrs. Evans," Jessica Ann said. "She has a parent-teacher conference with Mrs. Withers."

"Ah. You can wait in your classroom, if you like."

"Mommy asked me to meet her out front. I was just waiting for you to let the other kids out for their buses."

"I see. Well, that's just fine. Are you feeling better? I understand you were at the infirmary this morning."

"I just had a stomachache, Mrs. Evans. I'm okay now."

"Well, that's good." Mrs. Evans touched Jessica Ann's shoulder and squeezed gently.

Then Mrs. Evans wheeled away and, in a surprisingly loud, firm voice, called out for quiet, and the boisterous gym fell to relative silence and the first line of children moved out.

Jessica Ann trailed after the lineup for the bus she usually rode on, but as the kids streamed out of the front door, like wild animals suddenly uncaged, she kept a much slower pace than her peers. Her feet felt heavy. So did her shoulders, and her head. She didn't look at the white cotton-candy clouds moving above, only at their shadows gliding across her and the sidewalk her eyes were fixed upon.

It had been an excruciatingly long day for Jessica Ann. Knowing her mother was going to "reason" with Mrs. Withers about the Outstanding Student Award after school had made her physically ill. She hadn't gotten sick or anything, not in the throw-up way; just a really bad stomachache. And every time she looked up at Mrs. Withers, it got a little worse.

Her trip to the infirmary gave her an opening to ask to be sent home; but she didn't bother—she knew that wouldn't stop her mommy from seeing Mrs. Withers. Mommy wouldn't miss that meeting if bombs were dropping from the sky. So after some Pepto-Bismol and a half hour of almost napping on the cool crisp paper sheet of the infirmary bed, Jessica Ann told the school nurse she was ready to go back to class.

The afternoon had gone a little quicker—a history test had deflected her thoughts to schoolwork—and in fact time was suddenly moving too fast, the hand pointing to three and the bell ringing.

Now she was trudging down the sidewalk, amid the running, laughing, cheering kids, some lining up for their bus as Mrs. Evans oversaw their departure, others sailing by on bikes, still others being picked up by their parents.

As she neared the end of the sidewalk, a few yards

from the curb, she planted herself, sighed, and watched a happier world go by.

She saw blond little Lucy Peters, who was in Jessica Ann's class, getting picked up by her parents. Jessica Ann and Lucy had been the only kids in class to get A's on the science test, and Lucy was showing her mother her paper and getting a curbside hug that Lucy seemed embarrassed but not altogether displeased to receive. Lucy's father had come around from behind the wheel to open the side door of their van for his daughter; he was handsome, smiling, saying, "Nice job," and other encouraging, congratulatory stuff. He had on a jacket and tie; the mother was kind of dressed up, too, in a nice blue and white flower-print dress—were they going somewhere, as a family?

Jessica Ann wished she were Lucy, going with her pretty mommy and handsome daddy on some family outing.

Then Greg Meyers bumped into her, mumbling, "Sorry," and ran to the waiting arms of his big bearded grizzly bear of a dad and got a hug.

"I got picked for the track meet," Greg said.

"Way to go, buddy!" Greg's dad said; he was wearing a football jersey T-shirt and shorts, and reminded Jessica Ann of her late daddy. With his arm around his son, Greg's dad walked him across the street to where their car was parked.

Finally the last group of kids had piled onto the last bus, Mrs. Evans waving and heading back into the school, and as the vehicle pulled slowly away, wheezing and grinding like a weary beast, a figure standing there, waiting, was suddenly revealed, like an apparition materializing: Mommy.

Impeccable in a sensible yet stylish light tan suit with four bold buttons on a jacket sewn with a faint Spanish pattern, large flat white purse tucked under her arm, she strode forward, high heels clicking on concrete, the riddle of her well-chiseled features made an enigma by the big blank black lenses of her angular designer sunglasses and the high confident tilt of her chin. She didn't break her stride as she moved up to gather her waiting daughter, barely acknowledging the girl with the lightest glance, merely holding out her arm for Jessica Ann to slip into her grasp, which the child did, looking up at her mommy with gloomy resignation.

Soon mother and daughter were rounding the corner down the hallway that led to the fifth-grade classroom, Mommy slipping her sunglasses into her purse, Jessica Ann nervously playing with a pencil she'd withdrawn from her book bag when she sat waiting outside the front office, when Mommy stopped to check in with Mrs. Evans.

Halfway down the hallway, Miss Jones was cleaning the floor with mop and bucket, rather listlessly; the janitor, in white T-shirt (cigarette pack in the pocket) and jeans, a baseball cap snugged over her long stringy brown hair, was somebody kids at McKinley had long ago learned to steer clear of. Though not unattractive and only in her mid twenties, Miss Jones was known among Jessica Ann and her classmates as "the wicked old witch."

"Please don't do this, Mommy," Jessica Ann said, having to work a little to keep up with her mother, high heels click-clacking their way down the hall. "I don't want you to make Mrs. Withers mad at me."

"It's only a matter of what's fair, dear," Mommy said evenly. Then her voice turned cross: "You have better grades than that little . . ." She seemed to spit out the next word. ". . . *foreign* student."

"He's not foreign, Mommy," Jessica Ann said. "Eduardo is Hispanic, and he's a good student, too . . ."

"Not as good as you, dear."

Next to Mommy on the brick wall as she walked along were hanging papier-mâché tribal masks the fifth grade had made in Art, frightening demonic faces as disturbing as Mommy's was serenely madonnalike. The fourth grade had made the delicate pastel butterflies displayed along Jessica Ann's side of the hallway wall.

"The award is for Outstanding Student of the Year," Mommy was saying. "You have straight A's, perfect attendance. . . ."

"But, Mommy . . ."

They had caught up to Miss Jones, who had apparently not noticed them, and who made the mistake of getting in Mommy's way.

"Do you *mind*?" Mommy said contemptuously.

Miss Jones, a little surprised, her eyes hooded and sullen, lowered her head and mumbled, "Yes'um."

Then Miss Jones, pulling her mop and bucket

with her, stepped dutifully out of the way, and mother and daughter went on by. Jessica Ann glanced over her shoulder, and caught the janitor making a face at Mommy's back.

"No buts, dear," Mommy continued, unaware of this disrespect; lucky for Miss Jones. "Is that little Mexican in the 'Talented and Gifted' group? No!"

Jessica Ann sighed, shook her head, "It's just a stupid plaque. I don't need another."

"It's not a question of need, dear. It's a question of what's fair. Of what's right. Now . . ."

The splash of the mop and the rattle of the bucket signaled Miss Jones wheeling the tools of her trade into the janitor's station up the hall.

Mother and daughter were alone now, just outside the fifth-grade classroom.

". . . I think maybe this should be a private conference," Mommy whispered.

Desperate, Jessica Ann tried one last time to reason with her mother. "Mommy, *please* don't embarrass me."

Mommy seemed shocked, and maybe even a little hurt by this suggestion. "I would never do that," she said. Then her face blossomed into a lovely smile, and she tucked her hands behind her back, the purse in one of them. "Now. . . . Who's your best friend?"

Not again, Jessica Ann thought, sighing, "You are, Mommy."

Mommy covered her heart with a graceful hand, the red fingernails bold against the tan jacket. She shook her head regally and the scythes of her platinum hair shimmered as she said, "Who loves you more than anything on God's green earth?"

Jessica Ann glanced right and left to make sure no straggling classmates might catch a glimpse of this humiliating ritual.

Then she said, "You do, Mommy."

Mommy patted Jessica Ann's shoulder and pushed her gently along; doors to the outside waited at the end of the hall. "Now run along, dear, and I'll meet you on the playground."

"Yes, Mommy. . . ."

Jessica Ann shuffled down the hall, head down, defeated, her heart heavy.

Then Mommy's voice called out liltingly: "Jessica *Ann* . . ."

Hope leapt within her; had Mommy finally come to her senses? Had Jessica Ann actually gotten through to her Mommy? She turned, eyes wide and bright and hopeful. "Yes, Mommy?"

Mommy stood straight, pulling her shoulders back, and gave the child a gently reproving look. "Posture!"

And hope left her, like air from a punctured balloon. "Yes, Mommy. . . ."

Head hanging, the little girl trudged out to the playground, feet crunching across the gravel to the swing set where she deposited herself glumly in a swing and stared at the rocks.

And inside the school, her mommy entered the fifth grade classroom of Mrs. Withers.

* * *

Thelma Withers enjoyed decorating her classroom. She did it as much for herself as for the children; not only was it a creative outlet, but the sterile concrete-block classroom could always use some livening up.

Her favorite theme, and where she really tended to go overboard, was Christmas, touching childhood memories deep within her as it did—although this year, she had checked with Levi's parents first, to see if they objected, and they said as long as there were no "Christian symbols" displayed, it was okay with them. For that reason, she had avoided images of Santa Claus—technically, at least, he was "Saint Nicholas," after all.

Now, with Easter around the corner, she was happy to have the excuse of the upcoming Spring Fling—McKinley's annual carnivalstyle fund-raising event the night of the last big PTA meeting of the year—to drape her classroom with pink and yellow crepe paper, and staple her bulletin boards with colorful construction-paper tulips, birds, and balloons. She had decided against bunnies and eggs, because her students might feel too old for the easter bunny, and she wasn't anxious to invoke a religious holiday if she didn't have to.

She was proudest of her bulletin board headed "A Spring Bouquet," with a construction-paper bouquet's blossoms consisting of pasted pictures of the faces of children of various ethnic groups, clipped from magazines, smiling in a human array of colors and cultures. All around the bouquet of children, the word *Spring* was spelled out in lovely calligraphy in various languages—Spanish, French, Japanese, among others, except English.

The tall, big-boned teacher was on a stepladder stapling above the green chalkboard a computer printout banner with the words MCKINLEY SCHOOL SPRING FLING bracketed by flowers, when Mrs. Sterling's knock at the open door startled her.

Looking over her shoulder, grappling with the long, somewhat awkward-to-handle banner, Thelma Withers said, "Good afternoon, Mrs. Sterling. I hope you don't mind if I continue with my decorating. . . ."

The perfectly beautiful Mrs. Sterling, framed in the doorway, looked up at her with a frozen smile and frozen eyes; in her businesslike tan suit, she might have just come from the board meeting of some industry. Thelma Withers, in her black trousers and loose comfortable blouse with its bright multicolored geometric pattern, suddenly felt underdressed, as if she'd been caught at home in her pajamas.

Just the slightest annoyance could be heard in Mrs. Sterling's voice as she said, "We did have an appointment for a conference."

What a pain in the keister this woman was. Jessica Ann was a perfect student, and a wonderful little girl, if something of a case of arrested development, due to the smothering influence of her mother—what a monster! In almost thirty years of teaching, Thelma had never encountered the like of this one—constantly pestering her about imagined slights to her precious child.

Leaning against the top of the ladder, Thelma smiled down at the woman, trying to maintain a congenial tone. "Mrs. Sterling, we had our conference for the quarter just last week." She nodded toward the banner, which she was still trying to deal with, rather clumsily. "I'd like to get these decorations up, for the children—with the festival tomorrow night—"

"I was *wondering* why I didn't get a call to participate this year?" Mrs. Sterling asked crisply, still poised in the doorway. "I was in charge of the cakewalk last year, and we did quite well."

Thelma had been afraid this might come up. "May I be frank, Mrs. Sterling?"

Looking up placidly, Mrs. Sterling arched an eyebrow. "I hope you will be."

Thelma looked down at her sternly. "We had complaints about rudeness."

"Is that so?"

"It's so. You made catty remarks to several weight-challenged children."

Mrs. Sterling's mouth was a curving sarcastic line. "You mean, *fat* girls?"

Thelma winced; *God grant me patience*, she thought. "Three of them complained, and one of them was in tears."

Mrs. Sterling's expression was a mixture of shock and condescension. "You think it's a kind, responsible thing to do, giving some obese child a plate of pastry? I'm a mother with a daughter in this school, a daughter who happens to be one of McKinley's outstanding students, and I would like to have been paid the courtesy of being asked to help this year. If there's rudeness at question here, it was directed toward me."

Thelma sighed heavily. "Please . . . let's get not get off on the wrong foot, Mrs. Sterling." She stapled another section of the banner, shaking her head. "I really *do* want to have these decorations up for the children, and if you don't mind, we'll just talk while I work. . . ."

"I don't mind," the woman said coldly.

Moments later, Mrs. Sterling's voice came from the other side of the room: "You're presenting that plaque at the PTA meeting tomorrow evening. . . ."

Thelma hadn't even heard the woman walk to the desk, but there she was, lifting and then holding up the shining gold wall plaque for "Outstanding Student of the Year," staring at the plaque expressionlessly—yet there was something about the woman's eyes that told Thelma Withers just how covetous of the award she was.

"That's right, Mrs. Sterling," Thelma said, turning back to her work.

"You *know* that my daughter deserves that award."

Thelma turned to Mrs. Sterling and looked down at her with a smile. "Your daughter is a wonderful student . . ." And then she removed the smile and added: "But so is Eduardo Melindez."

And Thelma returned to her stapling.

Casually, Mrs. Sterling asked, "Are his grades as good as Jessica Ann's?"

Thelma stopped stapling and glanced back at the woman, literally looking down her nose at Jessica Ann's mother.

"Actually, Mrs. Sterling, that's none of your business. Neither is how I arrive at who the year's Outstanding Student is."

"Really."

"*Really*." Wasn't there any way to make this woman understand? "Mrs. Sterling, Eduardo faces certain obstacles your daughter does not. When someone like Eduardo excels, it's *important* to give him recognition. . . ."

"Because he's a Mexican?" The question was like a slap. And the amazed, self-righteous shock in the woman's face and voice seemed quite incredible to Thelma Withers. "You're punishing her for being white, and for coming from a good family?"

"I don't look at it that way," Thelma said, trying to sound reasonable, beginning to understand just how upset Mrs. Sterling was. "A person of color like Eduardo—"

Another slap of words, this time an interrupting one: "You're not going to give the award to Jessica Ann, are you?"

This *woman!* Disgusted, irritated beyond words, Thelma Withers tromped down the ladder, snatched the plaque from the woman's hands and tossed it on the desktop with a *thunk*.

Thelma's voice was as cold as Mrs. Sterling's eyes: "It's been decided."

Now Mrs. Sterling seemed to be the one trying to reason with an out-of-control woman. "There's no name on the plaque . . ."

"I'm dropping it off at the calligrapher's on the way home," Thelma said matter-of-factly, but rage was boiling within her.

Mrs. Sterling didn't seem to have heard her. "It's not too late for you to do the right thing."

"It is too late," Thelma said, making no attempt to conceal her cold disgust. "What are you *teaching* your daughter with behavior like this as an example?"

The beautiful face contorted into a sneer; the woman's rage seemed barely under control. Sarcasm-drenched words pelted the teacher: "What are *you* teaching her, when you take what's rightfully hers and give it to somebody because he's a 'person of color'?"

Thelma raised her hands as if to call an end to the proceedings. Then verbally she did just that: "I have nothing more to say to you, Mrs. Sterling. . . . Good afternoon."

And Thelma Withers went back to the ladder and clomped up to the top of it so she could get back to her stapling, which she did, teeth clenched, wishing she were stapling this awful woman's head to the wall.

The ladder shifted, suddenly, violently, and the teacher felt herself losing her balance . . .

Confused, afraid, dropping the stapler to the tile floor below with a *clunk*, she clawed for something to break her fall, something to hold onto, but caught only the banner, tearing it as she fell, and it drifted down with her, as she tumbled through the air and landed on her side with a hard *thud*, knocking the wind from her.

Moaning, wrapped in the banner saying SPRING FLING, Mrs. Withers opened her eyes, trying to push herself up. Her eyes were filled with the sight of Mrs. Sterling stepping around the toppled ladder, leaning in toward her, over her, her expression sympathetic, her two graceful hands extended as if to help her.

Chapter Seven

Jessica Ann, the only child on McKinley's little playground, hung onto the chain links of the swing and swung ever so gently, one toe poking gingerly at the tiny rocks below, careful not to scuff her beige flat. Even though as a fifth grader she was among the older kids in school, she was small for the swing, her petite bottom turning the U of the swing's rubber-strap seat into a V.

Like most children, Jessica Ann had scant sense of time. Five minutes, ten, half an hour, it was all the same, sheer boredom and floating thoughts. With the sun making its downward journey, the jungle gym, the curlicue slide, the monkey bars, and the rest were casting weird abstract shapes on the fine rocks of the playground bed. She watched the shadows lengthen and intertwine.

Consciously, she tried to move her thoughts away from Mommy confronting Mrs Withers. From time to time she would glance at the shade-drawn windows of her classroom, knowing Mommy and Mrs. Withers were in there talking, then shudder and look away and force herself to scoop a handful of rocks to look for agates or guess the color of the next car that moved down Kindler Avenue or give her mommy the count of ten to get out here and then when Mommy didn't get out here, give her another ten.

The playground brought back memories of her years at McKinley—though she'd almost never used any of these toys and couldn't remember ever sitting in one of these swings before—and she had a sudden pang of impending loss. Sixth grade would be at Central Middle School; she would be leaving McKinley soon, leaving the toys of childhood behind, whether she'd ever used them or not.

The sound of a rider mower greedily munching a lawn was interrupted by crunching footsteps on rock. Jessica Ann looked up sharply. Mommy—sunglasses on, purse tucked tightly under one arm—had rounded the corner of the school and was crossing the rocks of the playground bed. In her high heels, this took careful maneuvering, yet Mommy maintained her poise, her balance, her grace, not missing a single step.

Nonetheless, something was obviously wrong.

Mommy was frowning.

Not that Jessica Ann hadn't expected her mother

to be wearing a frown when she came out of the school. The child had been quite certain that not even Mommy would be able to change Mrs. Withers's mind about that award. But this was a special kind of frown, a fairly rare frown for Mommy's face, for it included no anger, merely concern, and Mommy's manner ever so barely betrayed something else rare for her: uneasiness.

As Mommy approached, removing her sunglasses, she gave Jessica Ann a sad little smile which seemed worse to the girl than the frown.

"Sorry I took so long, dear," her mother said.

The child was gripping the chain links of the swing. "Is . . . is something the matter?"

"Yes . . . there's been a terrible accident."

As she spoke, Mommy's eyes didn't seem to be able to land anywhere, particularly not on Jessica Ann, whose own eyes widened with alarm even as her heart began to race.

"When I went to speak to Mrs. Withers, she was lying on the floor . . ." Mommy gestured with a graceful open hand, her brow furrowing gravely as she seemed to be picturing the image as she described it to her daughter. ". . . she'd been up a ladder, decorating the room for you children."

"Oh, Mommy," Jessica Ann said. "Oh no. . . ."

Mommy nodded and looked skyward, reflectively. "She must have been a very . . . *thoughtful* teacher."

Jessica Ann felt as if she'd been hit in the pit of her stomach. "Mommy, you make it sound like she's . . ."

"Dead," Mommy said. "Yes, she's dead, dear."

Numbing shock hit Jessica Ann in a wave.

Mommy was shrugging, saying, "I think she may have broken her neck."

"Oh, Mommy," Jessica Ann whimpered, clutching the chains, and the child began to weep. Her mother stood close to her, but did not touch or comfort her daughter. Standing straight, purse tucked, she seemed to be setting a high standard of self-control and positive thinking in the face of tragedy.

In fact, she was explaining sweetly, "I stopped at the office and had the secretary phone for an ambulance. I'm afraid Mrs. Evans isn't taking this at all well. She doesn't appear to be a very strong woman." Mommy's expression signaled one of those rare occasions where she was soliciting Jessica Ann's opinion. "I think we should stay around, till help comes . . . don't you?"

"Y-yes, Mommy," the child managed.

And Mommy smiled, put on her sunglasses, and held out her hand. Together, mother and daughter tromped across the crunchy rocks and around to the front of the school.

"I called your Aunt Beth," Mommy said as they walked, "and asked her if she could come over and make us some dinner."

Jessica Ann said nothing.

"She said she could," Mommy continued.

Jessica Ann said nothing.

"Isn't that nice, dear?"

"Yes, Mommy."

An ambulance came very soon, its siren screaming: Jessica Ann covered her ears at what seemed to her the loudest, most unpleasant sound she'd ever heard. *What was their hurry?* she wondered irritably. *Why the rush? Hadn't anyone told them*?

Mrs. Withers was dead—what good would a doctor do?

Mrs. Evans, who had gotten her weeping under control finally, was waiting at the curb when the ambulance arrived and backed itself up in the bus loading zone; then two men in blue shirts and dark pants—they kind of looked like Boy Scouts, only a lot older—got a stretcher on wheels out of the back and rolled it up the long sidewalk and into the school.

Perhaps the ambulance attendants had read Jessica Ann's thoughts, because they didn't seem to be in any hurry.

The child and her mother stood in the shade of a small fully grown tree, off to themselves. A number of teachers were milling about out front, gathered in shocked little groups, shaking their heads, gesturing helplessly, this one weeping, that one comforting. Only Miss Jones, the janitor, didn't look very sad; she even had this kind of smirk, like something amusing had happened—now and then she'd check her watch, like she had someplace more important to get to.

Curbside, Mrs. Evans and a mustached man who Mommy said was the superintendent of schools were talking to two men, one of them a uniformed policeman, the other a red-faced brown-haired man in a suit and tie, who Mommy said she thought was a detective. Their police car, parked off to one side in the loading zone, had arrived without its siren on.

Finally, just as the afternoon was giving way to twilight, the doors of the school burst open as the ambulance attendants, one on either end, wheeled their stretcher down the long sidewalk. It was hard to imagine that long lumpy shape under the white sheet, held down with black straps, was Mrs. Withers. The teachers watching had expressions of sorrow and even horror, and yet they drew closer. Jessica Ann didn't want to get closer; she crossed her arms, hugging them to herself—it seemed so cold, suddenly.

"People die, dear," Mommy said, sunglasses on, chin up, purse tucked. She shrugged a little. "It's natural."

The ambulance attendants were putting Mrs. Withers in back of their vehicle, but Jessica Ann wasn't watching; she was looking at the patch of grass just in front of the toes of her beige Mary Janes, muttering, "What's so natural about falling off a ladder?"

Her mother whipped off the sunglasses and looked sharply at Jessica Ann, the china-blue eyes bearing down hard on the girl. "Is that a *smarty* tone?"

Jessica Ann drew back as if she'd been slapped. "No, Mommy!"

Mommy was shaking her head and her smile

wasn't really a smile. "Because I don't think Mrs. Withers would want you speaking to your mother in a smarty tone."

"No, Mommy."

Mommy turned away, facing the street, but she wasn't watching the ambulance, either, whose doors had just been shut; her gaze was distant. "Anyway . . . people fall off ladders all the time, *all* the time. As you know, dear, more accidents occur at home than anywhere else."

Careful to make sure her tone was respectful, Jessica Ann said, "But Mrs. Withers wasn't at home, Mommy."

"The workplace is the next most frequent."

The ambulance pulled away; no siren, this time. It passed a second police car pulling in, also without the siren going, though a certain sense of urgency was suggested when the policeman driving didn't even taken time to park, dropping off a small dark man with a snarl of dark hair and a sad, rumpled face. He must have been a detective, too, because he wore a silver gun with a square handle in a brown leather holster under his arm, though his clothes weren't neat like the other detective's: His shirt was blue and green and red and untucked, and he wore worn jeans and shoes with no socks. He was smoking a cigarette when he stepped out of the white and black police car, but pitched it away; he must have known the rule about smoking on school property.

The sloppy detective walked up to the tidy detective, who had a boyish face and a confused expression.

Jessica Ann couldn't hear what the two detectives said to each other, which was: "What are you doin' here, March? This is no homicide investigation."

"I'll get back to ya on that, Anderson. Where's our 'witness'?"

Jessica Ann didn't see the tidy detective pointing over at her and her mother, because she was looking up at Mommy, saying, "Can we go now?"

"No, dear," her mother said. "I'll need to speak to these gentlemen first."

And Mommy put on a very pleasant smile as the messy detective came over and introduced himself as Lieutenant March. He asked if they would mind going inside for a few moments, for some questions, and Mommy said she wouldn't mind in the least.

"Anything to be helpful, Lieutenant," she said.

Soon they were all sitting at tables in the school library. Jessica Ann was seated around the corner of a bookcase, by herself, but she could see her mother, seated at one end of a table, Lieutenant March at the other. A uniformed policeman stood by, like he was on guard duty. Mommy seemed perfectly at ease; she was self-composed and pleasant, while Lieutenant March slumped and sighed and grunted. He seemed a little grouchy, like maybe he didn't want to be there.

Jessica Ann didn't mean to eavesdrop, but Lieutenant March had a loud voice—and it got louder.

"So you didn't speak to Mrs. Withers *at all*?" he asked.

"How could I?" Mommy asked reasonably. "She was on the floor . . . with her neck broken."

He frowned at her, and there was impatience in his voice as he said, "But you had an *appointment*. . . ."

"Yes," Mommy said matter-of-factly. "A parent/teacher conference."

"Were you *on time* for the appointment?"

"I'm never late, Lieutenant," Mommy said. "Is there anything else?"

He heaved a sigh and put his notepad away. "No. Not right now, anyway."

"Thank you, Lieutenant," Mommy said, smiling radiantly, standing. "You have my address, my number . . . ?"

"Oh yeah," he said. He looked at her for what seemed like a long time. "I got your number."

Mommy didn't seem to notice the nasty look Lieutenant March was giving her as she moved away from the table; she was looking over at Jessica Ann, motioning for her to rise.

"Let's go, dear," Mommy said, tucking her purse tightly under her arm. "Your Aunt Beth is waiting dinner."

Jessica Ann met her mother halfway and Mommy slipped an arm around the girl's shoulder, guiding her out of the library as the sullen detective rose and followed them to the doorway.

Waiting just outside the library was that awful

Miss Jones. Mommy glanced at her, frowning just a little, before mother and daughter headed down the hall.

They heard Lieutenant March say to the janitor, "So . . . what's your story?"

And Mommy glanced back again, frowning again, as the detective and the janitor disappeared into the library.

"Is something wrong, Mommy?"

"No, dear. Everything's fine."

How could everything be fine, with Mrs. Withers dead?

Soon they were driving home in their blue Cadillac, with its I'M THE MOMMY, THAT'S WHY bumper sticker, and Mommy was humming a song that Jessica Ann didn't recognize. She supposed it was one of those really old songs Mommy liked, from the '70s or '80s.

Funny—her mother didn't seem very upset about Mrs. Withers at all. But then Mommy prided herself on a positive attitude.

Aunt Beth met them at the door, and she looked very upset—also very pretty, in a green sweater-blouse and full white skirt and that funky charm-bracelet necklace that Jessica Ann thought was really cool, only the girl wouldn't dare wear anything like that herself, because behind Beth's back Mommy had called it "tacky."

Jessica Ann trudged in, her book bag feeling heavy, the world feeling heavy, and suddenly Aunt Beth was all over her, bending down, putting her arm around her. She loved her Aunt Beth, but all this touching made her feel uneasy.

"You poor dear," Aunt Beth said. "Poor dear." She looked up at Mommy, worried. "Did she see . . . ?"

"No," Mommy said. "I discovered the body. Jessica Ann was on the playground."

"Thank God!" Aunt Beth said, then she looked searchingly from her sister's face to the little girl. "Do either of you even feel like eating?"

"Not really," Jessica Ann said.

Mommy gave the child a reproving look. "Now, Jessica Ann, your aunt was nice enough to come over here, at the last minute, and fix us some supper . . ."

"Don't worry about that," Aunt Beth said.

Mommy's expression brightened. "Smells like spaghetti."

"That's what it is," Aunt Beth said, smiling down at Jessica Ann, who wasn't fooled by the forced cheerfulness. "I made a big bowl of salad, too . . ."

"Can I just go to my room, please?" Jessica Ann asked, nodding toward the nearby stairway.

"No!" Mommy said. She raised a gently lecturing finger and looked sternly down at her daughter. "A little unpleasantness isn't going to stand in the way of good nutrition."

Aunt Beth was frowning, but it was a sad frown. "Please . . . if she doesn't want—"

Mommy gave Aunt Beth the "mind your own business" look. Aunt Beth, who'd had many of these looks from her sister over the years, glanced away with a hurt, faint, frustrated frown.

Then Mommy turned to Jessica Ann, and pointed to the kitchen, which the entryway opened onto, taking the girl's book bag from her, nudging her gently toward the waiting table, perfectly set by Aunt Beth. "Now, march in there, young lady."

"Yes, Mommy. . . ."

"Your salad, too!"

"Yes, Mommy."

Jessica Ann sat at the table, folded her hands, saying her prayers. She didn't hear the whispered conversation between her mother and Aunt Beth.

"I take it you called Mark, and that he'll be over."

"Yes," Beth said.

"I didn't imagine you'd gussied yourself up for Jessica Ann and me."

"Sis, I'm *not* interested in Mark—"

"Beth, I'm just teasing."

"Well, he can't make it for dinner, still had work to do at his office. He said he could have dessert with us later. I told him about today . . ."

"Good. He's a positive influence on Jessica Ann. He'll calm her down."

"She doesn't need calming down, she needs understanding."

"Beth, with all due respect, you run your little preschool your way, and I'll raise my daughter mine. Understood?"

"Yes. . . ."

"And one other little thing." She thrust her finger

in Beth's face as if pointing a pistol, and sudden rage filled her harshly whispered words: "Don't you *ever* contradict me in front of my daughter again."

Beth drew back as if the door on a blast furnace had suddenly been opened on her.

Then, seeming to catch herself, her sister added, in a much more reasonable tone, "You know how impressionable young girls can be."

And Jessica Ann's mother, with her daughter's book bag in hand, went up the steps to freshen up for supper, and for Mark.

Chapter Eight

After dinner, Jessica Ann went up to her room and got into some more comfortable clothes—a white top with a pretty floral pattern at its turtleneck, crisp new Guess jeans and white Reeboks; even comfy, she wanted to look nice for Mark—and she knew her mommy would expect that of her, anyway.

Much as she adored Mark, Jessica Ann didn't rush down when she heard what she thought was his little red Porsche pull up. Or when she heard somebody come in downstairs, probably Mark, but the voices were muffled, and Jessica Ann just couldn't move off the bed. It was like she was paralyzed or maybe hypnotized.

She lay on her back on the bed, her little elbows winged out, staring at the swirls of the textured ceiling, getting lost in them, working to make her eyes and mind swim. Which was so much better than thinking. . . .

The child hadn't eaten much at the table, and neither Mommy nor Aunt Beth complained; she felt sick to her stomach, nauseated almost, and even Aunt Beth's famous family spaghetti sauce didn't go down right.

On her desk was her book bag, where homework in three subjects awaited; normally her pattern was to hit the books right after supper, so she could watch a little TV and do some reading before bed. But she couldn't seem to drag herself off the bed to do it.

All she could think of was Mrs. Withers, and how nice she was, and how she was dead now.

Turning on her side, she drew her teddy bear to her and tried not to cry, but she just couldn't help it, and pretty soon Teddy was damp with her tears.

A knock at her bedroom door drew her attention, and she turned toward the sight of a gently smiling Aunt Beth, cracking the door open, peeking in. "Jessy—mind if I come in?"

The child shook her head no, sitting up a little, the pillows behind her providing support, and she reached for several tissues from the pink box on her nightstand, next to Daddy's framed picture. It embarrassed Jessica Ann to be caught like that, bawling like a little baby.

Aunt Beth sat on the edge of the bed, right up beside her niece, bodies touching as she leaned in intimately, touching Jessica Ann's forearm.

"Don't feel bad about crying," Aunt Beth said. "It's good to get it out of your system."

Jessica Ann dabbed at the tears with the tissue. "Do . . . do you think Mrs. Withers had any children?"

"Probably," Aunt Beth said. "Maybe even grandchildren."

"Do you . . . do you think I should write them a letter?"

That seemed to puzzle Aunt Beth a little. "Why, dear?"

Jessica Ann swallowed. "To tell them about what a good teacher she was. . . ."

Then Jessica Ann's tears began to flow again and Aunt Beth, whose smile seemed suddenly even more beautiful than Mommy's but whose eyes had filled up with tears, too, drew Jessica Ann to her, tightly but tenderly, patting her back in a "there, there" fashion. This time Jessica Ann didn't mind Aunt Beth's getting "touchy-feely" (as Mommy put it). She squeezed back, crying into her aunt's shoulder.

Finally, the two drew apart, but remained in each other's arms; Jessica Ann felt a closeness to her aunt that really seemed to help the hurt.

"I think writing Mrs. Withers's children is a wonderful idea," Aunt Beth said. "Do you want me to find out what their names are?"

"Would you, Aunt Beth?"

"Absolutely."

Jessica Ann dabbed away the new tears with the

old tissue. "I'll write it tonight," she said, "and add their names later."

Aunt Beth nodded, smiling her sad smile.

"Do you think Mommy's upset about . . . what happened?"

"I'm sure she is, dear."

"She doesn't seem to be."

"Remember our talk, Jess? After Mr. Sterling died? About how Mommy was a 'special' person . . . ?"

"Yes." Jessica Ann swallowed, glancing over at the I ♥ DADDY framed photo. "But sometimes I don't think Mommy misses either one of them . . . Daddy *or* Mr. Sterling."

Aunt Beth's brow furrowed. "Jessy . . . do you cry in front of your mommy?"

"No!"

"If you're sad, you . . . you keep it to yourself, don't you?"

"I guess."

"How do you know your mommy doesn't cry herself to sleep at night? We can't ever know, not ever really know, what's in the heart of another person."

"You think Mommy . . . hides her feelings?"

"That's very possible."

Jessica Ann sighed. "She sure does a good job."

That seemed to stop Aunt Beth cold for a second.

But then her aunt said, "You know, speaking of your mother . . . she had a chocolate cake already baked for this evening." Aunt Beth arched an eyebrow, giving the girl a sly half-smile. "Of course, I suppose you're too *blue* for chocolate cake. . . ."

Suddenly Jessica Ann didn't feel nauseated at all. And nobody made rich, "sinful" desserts better than her mommy.

Was it disrespectful to Mrs. Withers's memory to eat a piece of cake? Jessica Ann couldn't be sure, but if she'd learned one thing in her young life, it was, "Life goes on."

"Is Mark here?" the girl asked, perking up. "I thought I heard him come in. . . ."

"Right downstairs," Aunt Beth said, smiling. "And he's been asking for you."

"Really?"

"What do you think, Jess?" Aunt Beth's smile had lost its sadness. "Mark and chocolate cake," she said. "Now, there's a combo few girls could resist."

Jessica Ann beamed, withdrew a final tissue from the box on her nightstand, dried her eyes, took her aunt's hand, and allowed herself to be led out of her room and down the stairs.

Halfway down, at the landing, Jessica Ann spotted Mark, sitting in the chair by the phone, the chair Mommy sat in after Mr. Sterling's funeral. He was reading the paper, with it folded over so he could hold it in one hand, while he held a glass of iced tea in the other, sipping it occasionally.

He must have heard them coming down, because he lowered the paper and put the iced tea on the end table next to him, smiling over at Jessica Ann and Aunt Beth, who had paused at the landing; it was not the kind of smile a kid got from most grown-ups—it was the smile of somebody sincerely, honestly happy to see you.

And it filled Jessica Ann with joy.

"*There's* my girl!" he said, and put the paper aside, tossing a little wave at Aunt Beth, who smiled shyly and waved back, heading on into the kitchen.

Jessica Ann was almost running toward him, till he held out his arms for her . . . and then she felt suddenly embarrassed, stopping in her tracks. She leaned against the post of the divider where the phone sat, and smiled at him and waved a timid hello.

"Well, come on!" he said, still smiling big, motioning her over. There was no refusing such a direct, loving command, and she scurried over and climbed in his lap.

Mark was younger than either Mr. Sterling or Daddy, and really good looking, like a soap opera actor with his dark hair and nice tan and neatly trimmed beard. He wore a white shirt and dark slacks and a gold watch that looked expensive. And he smelled so good, like the outdoors, like a forest. . . .

He held her as she sat on his knee like a kid giving Santa her wish list, then his smile tightened into something serious, and he studied her, which made her feel a little awkward. "Are you okay, angel?"

"Sure."

"Your mommy told me about today." He made a *tch* sound, shook his head once. "Awful rough."

She shrugged.

Then he twitched a smile as he eased her off his lap, taking her hand, saying, "Step into my office. . . ."

And he guided her over to the couch, saying, "Angel, if you ever need somebody to *talk* to . . ."

They were seated now, but he was turned sideways, looking right at her. She turned to look at him, folding her hands in her lap.

"I'm fine, Mark," she said again, then emphatically added, "*Real*-ly."

He leaned forward, and his voice was soft, soothing yet strong. "You know . . . when I was ten, my Boy Scout leader died. . . . He was killed in an automobile accident. And I didn't have a dad around . . . he and Mom were divorced . . . and that Scout troop leader kind of became a . . . surrogate father to me. Do you know what that means?"

She nodded, reached for and took his hand, which seemed to surprise him, but in a nice way. "Kind of took the place of your real dad?"

"That's right," he said, nodding, smiling, patting her hand. "That's right. . . . Anyway, after he died, I felt . . . empty." The smile faded. "And then I started to feel afraid. . . ."

"Afraid?"

He nodded again. "And for the first time, I started to think about dying. I had trouble sleeping. I had nightmares. And for the first time I realized that . . . nobody lives forever."

Mark was so sweet. But Jessica Ann had known about people dying for a long time.

"Anyway," he said, patting her hand, "if you ever have any trouble like that . . . I just wanted you to know, I'm here for you."

She didn't say anything—just beamed at him.

Aunt Beth came in from the kitchen through the dining room and knelt down before them. "Who's for dessert?"

Mark gave Jessica Ann an intense look, then blurted, "I am!"

"I am!" Jessica said, raising her hand and waving, and followed her aunt back to the kitchen, Mark bringing up the rear.

As they moved through the kitchen, Mommy was at the counter that divided the work area from the dining area. She was slicing a double-layer, cherry-topped chocolate cake with a big shiny knife; the way the red cherry topping clung to the knife made it look like blood and Jessica Ann thought, *Gross!*, but it didn't stop her from digging in when her mommy put a nice big slice down in front of her at the table.

Mark was sitting right across from Jessica Ann, who nibbled at her cake and watched him adoringly. Maybe it wasn't right, so soon after Mr. Sterling died, but she hoped Mommy would marry Mark. She didn't think it would be hard to call *him* "Daddy."

And Mommy was certainly catering to her new boyfriend. Right now she was handing him a piece of cake so big, it made the hunk Jessica Ann had been served look like a sliver.

"Whoa!" he said, taking the plate, reacting comically as if it weighed a ton. "Kill me with kindness. . . ."

"I like to spoil my children," Mommy said, looking from Mark to Jessica Ann.

Her mother looked especially beautiful tonight, her platinum hair pinned up and back in a French twist, accenting her high cheekbones, pink imitation pearls caressing the lovely lines of her neck, her shapely figure well-served by the lavender silk pants with matching tunic, protected by an old-fashioned lacy apron (Mommy always wore aprons in the kitchen, even though she never got anything on them).

But most of all, Mommy's eyes were beautiful, those china-blue eyes which so often had a coldness about them seemed to take on a sparkle around Mark, with smile lines providing an attractive setting for such precious gems.

Ever since her mother met Mark at the country club dance last February—Jessica Ann had heard Mommy say Mark had moved to Ferndale to get away from the "urban blight" where he used to live—Mommy had been happier than her daughter could remember.

Jessica Ann didn't know if Mommy had ever been happy with Mr. Sterling; the two of them had seemed to get along okay, and it was only those few months before Mr. Sterling died that Jessica Ann remembered hearing the muffled sounds of arguments coming up from downstairs. Mommy had acted affectionate around Mr. Sterling, but around Mark, Mommy seemed different—loving, even.

Maybe that was because Mark wasn't old, like Mr. Sterling. Even Daddy had been old, not as old as Mr. Sterling, but lots older than Mommy. He had left them "well off" (as Mommy put it), though a few times Jessica Ann heard Mommy talking with Aunt Beth about Daddy's "bad investments"—fortunately Mr. Sterling had come along about the time Daddy's money ran out.

Anyway, Mark wasn't old like Daddy and Mr. Sterling—though he was kind of rich, she gathered, from some kind of mail-order thing—and maybe that was why Mommy seemed to feel different about him than about the others.

Right now Mommy—the only one not yet seated at the table, but poised over her chair, next to Mark—was about to hand a piece of the cake to Jessica Ann to pass to Aunt Beth.

"I'll just have the ice cream," Aunt Beth told Mommy with a forced little smile.

Mommy had already served everyone with a separate bowl of ice cream.

"What's *wrong* with me?" Mommy said. "You're allergic to chocolate! How stupid of me."

"Don't be silly. . . ."

Mommy's smile was beguiling; her eyes promised delight. "How about some strawberry compote on that ice cream?"

Aunt Beth beamed at her sister's thoughtfulness. "Oooo . . . that does sound good."

Mommy sat down. "There's a jar in the fridge," she said curtly.

Aunt Beth's smile turned into a smirk and she shook her head. She rose and went to the refrigerator, but when she brought the jar back to the table, she struggled to screw open its lid, without success.

"Here," Mark said, reaching out, "let me have a crack at that. . . ."

And he took the jar from her, but he must not have been as strong as he looked; he just couldn't budge the lid.

"Criminey," he said, still trying.

"Here," Mommy said impatiently, gesturing for him to hand her the jar, which he did, and with a quick thrust, she opened the lid with a loud *pop* that startled everybody.

Mark seemed particularly amazed, studying Mommy for a moment, then grinning across at Jessica Ann as Mommy handed him the jar to pass along to Aunt Beth. "Your mommy's pretty strong for a girl."

"Now, there's a sexist remark," Mommy said, half-kidding, and Mark raised his hands in apologetic surrender.

"I've seen her do that," Jessica Ann said, "with pickle jars and ketchup bottles, lots of times."

Mark considered this information, and said to Mommy, "Remind me not to cross you."

Mommy shrugged. "Don't cross me," she said, and then she looked at Mark lovingly and smiled her dazzling smile.

Chapter Nine

The next morning, Mrs. Evans introduced Miss Morrison, the substitute teacher, to the fifth-grade class. The principal also announced that Mrs. Withers's funeral would be tomorrow, Friday, and this was followed by a rumbling murmur that rolled across the classroom in a wave—the playground rumor had been that the whole school would be dismissed so that those children who wanted to could attend.

Of course, there had also been a rumor that an electrical-tape body outline where Mrs. Withers fell would be on the floor in the classroom when they got there this morning, and that had proved false.

"People!" Mrs. Evans said, her tone firm but her voice quavery. "Please. Mrs. Withers's family is holding a small, private service for family and close friends. There will be visitation this evening . . ."

And the principal wrote the name and address of the funeral home on the chalkboard, as she continued talking.

". . . from six until eight. Please tell your parents. Also, Mrs. Withers's family requested that, in lieu of flowers, memorial donations may be made to UNICEF."

And Mrs. Evans wrote that address down, too. About a third of the kids, Jessica Ann among them, dutifully copied down the information.

The substitute teacher, Miss Morrison, was tall and slender and pretty and young, with long dark hair pinned up in a French twist like Mommy's last night, and a flower-pattern vest over a white blouse, and a long white skirt. Mrs. Withers never wore feminine clothes like that and, of course, had been much older. The class immediately took to Miss Morrison, and at the first recess there was much talk of how nice she was and how pretty.

Jessica Ann knew that her classmates meant no disrespect to their late teacher; they were just relishing a change of pace coming, so late in the school year. If anything, Jessica Ann was relieved by this warm reception, because substitute teachers—particularly young, obviously inexperienced ones like Miss Morrison—could just as easily be the target of a campaign of juvenile terrorism—books dropped collectively at a certain designated times, variation from the seating chart, and derisive comments when the teacher's back is turned at the chalkboard.

And Miss Morrison was obviously nervous, even with so benign a response from the thirty kids of this fifth-grade class. Her large brown eyes had the beauty—and the terror—of a doe caught in headlights. Jessica Ann liked her, and felt sorry for her.

When Mrs. Evans came to the door just before the afternoon study period, and called Miss Morrison out into the hall, Jessica Ann hoped the substitute teacher wasn't in trouble. The momentarily unattended classroom had its first cathartic burst of substitute-teacher reaction in a sudden storm of paper airplanes, spitballs, and note-passing, which immediately abated on Miss Morrison's return.

Miss Morrison sat at her desk and organized things for a while, checking the little faces on her seating chart; then she looked up at Jessica Ann, sitting right in front, almost directly across from the teacher's desk, and said, "Step out into the hall with me, please, Jessica Ann."

A sudden murmur passed across the class, getting them their first rebuke of the day from Miss Morrison: "Quiet!" The students hadn't meant disrespect, but were merely reacting in surprise—once again, the best-behaved girl in class, perhaps in school, was being asked out into the hall where scoldings were the rule.

Outside the classroom, Miss Morrison slipped her arm around Jessica Ann's shoulder. "Mrs. Evans asked me to send you down to her office."

"Am I in trouble?"

"No. They just want to talk to you about Mrs. Withers."

"What *about* Mrs. Withers?"

"She didn't say, Jessica Ann. Now, run along. . . ."

"Oh-kay," Jessica Ann sighed.

What could Mrs. Evans want with her? What did Jessica Ann know about Mrs. Withers's death? Nothing! Mrs. Withers was already dead when Mommy got there; was already dead when Jessica Ann and her mommy were walking down this very hall, in the other direction.

Down at the far end it loomed: the principal's office. That was where bad kids went. In all her years of grade school, she'd never been called there, never been in trouble. She trudged down the hallway, watching her Mary Janed feet, listening to her own footsteps, hearing them echo. So strange to be out here while class was in session, the muffled classroom sounds behind each door, and just empty, echoey silence out here.

Something flopped in front of her, making a wet splashy *slap* on the tile floor. The soaked gray tendrils of a mop, tangled in a sodden wad, splashed her shoes.

She hopped back and said, "Hey!"

Stepping in front of the girl's path, emerging from the janitor's station like a creature from its cave, sluggish but dangerous, came Miss Jones—Miss Jones in her sweaty untucked T-shirt with the cigarette pack in its pocket, with the baseball cap pulled down over straggly brown hair whose tendrils were as tangled as her mop's, Miss Jones with her spooky bulgy brown eyes and her gum-chewing smirk, looming over the child, extending her arm with the mop handle so that Jessica Ann's way was blocked.

"What's the matter?" Miss Jones asked. Her voice had a nasty, lazy quality, like she was caressing each unwilling word. "Little Miss Perfect get called to the principal's office?" She made a *tch-tch* sound and shook her head in mock sympathy, even while she kept the pathway blocked with her extended arm, mop handle in hand, trapping the girl against the lockers.

"You mind your own business," Jessica Ann huffed, standing up to the woman. She was afraid of the janitor, but didn't think of Miss Jones in the way she did most adults; Miss Jones was more like another child—a big mean child who just happened to be about twenty-five.

"Will you please get out of my way?" Jessica Ann said, chin firm, eyes hard. "Mrs. Evans is waiting."

"Oh, I know all about that," the janitor said, casually taunting, even as she looked the girl up and down in a leering fashion that Jessica Ann found particularly creepy. "And I know somethin' *you* don't, Little Miss Silver Spoon."

It was Jessica Ann's turn to sneer. "You don't know anything."

The janitor leaned in close; her breath smelled like cigarettes. "I know there's some policemens waiting to talk to *you*."

Jessica Ann's heart leaped to her throat. "What?"

Now the janitor, relishing having the upper hand, began to smile, and she moved her head from side to side, like she was trying to be cool. "Maybe they wanna ask you what your mama was doin' in Miss *Withers's* room yesterday."

What a stupid woman.

"Everybody knows what my mother was doing in Mrs. Withers's room," Jessica Ann said, her patience strained. "She found the body."

The janitor's eyebrows climbed high over the bulging eyes. "Maybe I seen your mama go in there and stay for a good, long while. . . ." She leaned closer and whispered nastily, "Maybe I heard 'em *talkin'* in there. . . ."

"You didn't see anything."

Miss Jones leaned in so close that Jessica Ann reared back. "I see everything that goes on around this place." She lifted her chin and her eyes seemed huge and scary. "Nothin' gets past *these* eagle eyes."

Anger bubbled up through Jessica Ann's fear and she got right in the janitor's face, standing up for herself and her mommy. "You're a *liar*! And my minister says liars go to *hell*!"

Now it was the janitor who reared back, startled by the little girl's vehemence and insolence, and she indignantly cried, "Don't you go talkin' to me like that! I'm . . . I'm like a *teacher*! You can't—"

A sudden hand on the janitor's shoulder pulled her away from Jessica Ann, startling both of them. It was Mrs. Jensen, the assistant principal, a dark-haired lady in her forties who was usually very nice but right now had a terribly cross expression.

"Jones!" she barked. "Get back to your work."

"Yes'um," Miss Jones muttered, hunkering down over her mop, as if she were trying to make herself smaller.

"Jessica Ann," Mrs. Jensen said, lifting her chin, looking sternly at the girl, "move along."

But Jessica Ann thought she heard Miss Jones laughing to herself as she hunched over the mop, working at a rate that wouldn't get the hall cleaned in a month.

The tidy-looking policeman was standing outside the principal's office, as if he were a big kid summoned there. He moved to one side as Mrs. Evans stepped out to meet Jessica Ann, and her smile was warm; she slipped her arm around the girl's shoulder and said, "There's a gentleman who'd like to speak to you. If you're uncomfortable, I want you to know you can leave at any time."

"Y-yes, ma'am."

The principal's frown was kindly. "I'm doing this reluctantly, and normally I would require this interview to be held in your mother's presence."

"Interview?"

Mrs. Evans gazed at the girl, her manner reassuring. "But I'm told this will be informal, and brief, and as I say, you can leave when you like—I'll be waiting here in the outer office."

They stepped inside, and through the open door of Mrs. Evans's office, Jessica Ann could see him, seated at Mrs. Evans's desk, waiting: that policeman who had asked the loud, rude questions of Mommy, that detective in the messy clothes with the dark sad face.

He saw Jessica Ann, too, and rose and put a smile on the sad face, coming out to meet the child and her principal. He wore an untucked off-white sport-shirt with the brown holster and gun over it, and faded blue jeans.

"You remember me, Jessica Ann?" he asked, still smiling, gesturing to himself. "I'm Lieutenant March."

"Yes, sir."

He bent toward her. "Now, Mrs. Evans has given us permission to use her office. . . ."

Mrs. Evans confirmed this with a nod to Jessica Ann.

"Could we talk for a while, Jessica Ann?" the policeman asked. He seemed as nice today as he'd been grouchy yesterday.

"Okay."

Mrs. Evans turned the child over to the policeman, who guided the girl gently into the principal's cramped office, ushering her to a chair near the desk. Jessica Ann had never been in Mrs. Evans's office before; though small, it was bright and cheerful, with colorful educational posters on the walls and a big cloth decorative multicolor likeness of a hot air balloon hanging on the side of a filing cabinet. Jessica Ann wished she could climb aboard the balloon and fly away somewhere, anywhere but here in this cheerful, terrible little office.

Lieutenant March didn't get behind Mrs. Evans's desk: He knelt down next to Jessica Ann as she sat, so when she looked at him he was at her eye level. He was leaning against the metal arm of the chair, and maybe he meant it to be friendly or cozy or something. But Jessica Ann felt hemmed in, and almost as trapped as she had by Miss Jones out in the hall.

"Jessica Ann . . ." He had a mellow, deep, soothing voice, only his words weren't soothing at all. ". . . why did your mother want to see Mrs. Withers yesterday?"

"They had a conference."

He nodded. "Ah yes, a parent/teacher conference."

"Yes, sir."

Another smile, half a smile, anyway. "You don't have to call me 'sir,' Jessica Ann." He dug a roll of Life Savers from his pocket and offered her one.

"No thank you."

"You sure?"

"Mommy says not to take candy from strangers."

"I don't want us to be strangers, Jessica Ann," the policeman said. "I want us to be friends."

"Friend or stranger," Jessica Ann said, "candy rots your teeth, Mommy says."

Lieutenant March sighed, popped a Life Saver in his mouth, and got to his feet, patting the child's head, a gesture she drew away from—she didn't like being *touched* by strangers, either.

"Maybe your mommy doesn't always know best," the policeman said.

She didn't say anything.

He settled himself into Mrs. Evans's chair now, and leaned back in it, rocking a little; he was still smiling, a forced smile she didn't entirely believe, particularly since his eyes weren't smiling at all as he appraised the child across the desk.

"Jessica Ann," he said finally, "do you know how your teacher died?"

"Fell off a ladder."

"She did fall off a ladder, yes," he said, and laughed silently, to himself. What was funny about that? "But Jessica Ann . . . your teacher . . . died of a broken neck . . ."

"When she fell off the ladder."

Her matter-of-fact monotone replies were obviously not giving the policeman much satisfaction, and his smile shifted again, into the kind of smile Aunt Beth had had last night after Mommy told her the strawberry compote was in the refrigerator.

"Now, we have a man called a Medical Examiner," Lieutenant March said, "who says that it didn't happen like that." And he shook his head to emphasize his point, and then he held his hands up and made claws of them. "He says it's very likely a pair of *hands* did it."

Maybe it was because Jessica Ann had just thought of it, but suddenly the image of the jar of strawberry compote filled her mind's eye, the image of her mommy's strong hands twisting the lid off ever so easily with an awful *pop*.

Then the image was gone, and the child swallowed, and calmed herself, and sank further down in the chair, trying to disappear. The colorful cloth balloon was just behind Lieutenant March's head. She looked past him at it, dreaming she was on it, wishing his words would go away.

But they didn't, although his attempt to smile had. "Jessica Ann . . . something was missing from Mrs. Withers's desk."

"Could I please go?" she asked, shifting uneasily in her chair. "My stomach hurts. . . ."

"It was a plaque, Jessica Ann . . . for the 'Outstanding Student of the Year,' an honor that I understand you won, last year? Hmmm?"

She sighed. "Yes, sir."

"There's that 'sir' again," he said, back to the unconvincing smile. "Now . . . Mrs. Withers told several friends that your mother called her, complaining about you not winning this year."

The child shrugged, just barely. "She thought I deserved to win."

"I'm sure you did," he said quickly, "I'm sure you did. But, Jessica Ann . . . the mother of the boy who won the plaque, Eduardo's mother, uh, Mrs. Melindez? I'm sure she'd love to have that plaque. Would mean a lot to her."

She turned away from his gaze.

"If you should happen to find it . . . would you tell me?"

Now she looked right at him; anger was starting to bubble up again. "Why would *I* find it?"

Lieutenant March shrugged. "I don't know . . . you just might. Maybe your mother picked it up, as she went out of the classroom—"

"Who *says* she did?" Jessica Ann demanded.

Her frown made the policeman back up a little, and he raised his hands in a defensive manner. "Nobody . . ."

"And, anyway, that wouldn't prove anything."

The policeman frowned, too, but it was thoughtful not angry. "Who said anything about *proving* anything, Jessica Ann?"

The girl stood up jack-in-the-box quickly, and it seemed to startle Lieutenant March. Then she patted the desktop, once, like she was swatting a disobediant child, and her chin crinkled with determination and indignation.

She said, "I think if you have any more questions for me, Lieutenant March, you should talk to my mother *first*."

He smiled again, gesturing. "Jessica Ann . . ."

But the girl didn't hear anything else, not anything the policeman said, or anything any of her friends said the rest of the afternoon, or Miss Morrison, either.

All she could hear was the sound of the strawberry compote jar, making its awful *pop* as Mommy twisted off its lid.

Chapter Ten

The only kind of bad thing about Miss Morrison was that she had assigned them a lot of homework, like she was trying to prove to them that she was really a teacher.

So Jessica Ann got an early start on it as soon as she got home from school, sitting at the kitchen table where the light came in so nicely through the big fern-plant-bordered windows.

"You *are* a good girl," Mommy said, noticing what her daughter was up to. "Let me get you some milk and cookies. Or would you rather have an apple?"

"Milk and cookies, please."

Soon Mommy was setting a big glass of milk and a plate of cookies next to Jessica Ann, but the plate had only three small cookies on it—suppers didn't get spoiled in the Sterling house—and then Mommy got behind the big counter to make herself some coffee, taking a jar of instant off the shelf. It was a brand-new jar and when Mommy opened it, the vacuum pop made Jessica Ann jump . . . and reminded her, again, of the strawberry compote jar. She frowned and dug into her homework. *If Jaspar had twelve bushels of corn, and his neighbor Efram had . . .*

"How was school today, dear?" Mommy asked, spooning the instant into an empty coffee cup.

"Okay," Jessica Ann said, erasing a mistake.

"Anything special happen?"

She blew eraser crumbs away from the page. Should she tell her mother? Maybe she should.

"I talked to that policeman," Jessica Ann said, redoing the multiplication.

"What policeman?"

She shrugged, trying to concentrate on the problem.

"Lieutenant March?"

She nodded, continuing her work.

Mommy was pouring hot water from a teapot into the coffee cup. "What did he want, dear?"

"He just asked some questions."

"Oh? About what, dear?"

"You know . . . about Mrs. Withers."

Steam rose in front of Mommy's face. "What did he want to know, dear?"

"Just about the award and stuff. I didn't talk to him very long. I said if he wanted to talk to me he should get your permission."

"Sounds like you handled yourself very well, dear. . . ."

"I just hope . . . nothing."

"What, dear?"

Jessica Ann sighed heavily. "I just hope he doesn't talk to Miss Jones."

"*Who*, dear?"

Jessica Ann shuddered at the memory of the hallway confrontation with that cigarette-breath monster. "That *awful* janitor. She was teasing me and saying terrible things."

"Oh?" Mommy couldn't have sounded less concerned or more casual. "Like what, dear?"

"That you were in Mrs. Withers's room a long time, talkin' to her."

Mommy didn't respond at first, and Jessica Ann thought the conversation was over, and that she could at last begin to concentrate on these math problems.

Then suddenly Mommy said, in a harsh judgmental tone Jessica Ann was all too familiar with, though it had rarely been leveled her way, "She's a stupid woman in a menial job. Ignore her."

"Yes, Mommy."

"Uggh!"

Jessica Ann turned to look at her mommy, who was making a face over the lip of the coffee cup. "How I *hate* this instant. . . ."

Mommy began to pace back behind the counter, tugging at her pearls, and at the scoop neck of her lovely blue dress.

"We're out of everything in this house," Mommy said, then she halted her pacing, a decision made. "Maybe I should make a run to the store, and get some fresh-ground."

Jessica Ann turned all the way around in the chair, asking brightly, "Can I go along?"

She loved to shop with Mommy, helping pick out meals and snacks and stuff.

Mommy thought over her daughter's request for a moment, then smiled enchantingly and said, "Why don't you just stay here and finish your homework. Then maybe later we can watch a video."

"Great!"

Mommy was gathering the car keys and her purse. "I'll swing by Video Warehouse. . . . How 'bout *Beauty and the Beast* again?"

"Excellent!"

Jessica Ann got back to work as her mother left the house. This was a rare treat—a video on a school night! And a sign that Mommy was finally starting to think of Jessica Ann as responsible enough to stay at home, alone, without calling a sitter or at least Aunt Beth. How embarrassing it was to her, at an age when her peers were taking baby-sitting jobs themselves, to be baby-sat.

Maybe Mommy was changing, and for the better.

Leann Jones had been one of McKinley's two full-time maintenance engineers for three years. She knew the job was beneath her potential—she just wasn't sure what her potential was, or anyway where it lay. She was neither happy nor unhappy in her job, it was just something she'd put in for, and got, and did. The pay was better than waitressing and the medical plan was good.

Chris, her significant other, had a good job at the grain-processing plant, good pay, nice benies, except for that damn swing shift, and they were talking about selling the trailer and buying a little house.

Of course, with those kind of bills to pay, that meant Leann would have to keep this lousy job, or find another. Not that maintenance at McKinley was hard, though it did have its unpleasant side, like cleaning up puke, which some kid somewhere in the school managed to do at least once a week. Sometimes the scent of vomit and sawdust came home with her to the point where she couldn't even stand to eat, much less do the microwaving herself.

She wasn't ambitious, though it probably would have surprised her to know that. She felt secretly superior to people, as if, were she ever to have the inclination to bust out of her shell, would *they* be in trouble. Her idea of a good time was a night out—the Golden Spike with its live country music was her bar of choice—or a quiet night at home with Chris and a six-pack or maybe some weed. Life was mostly a pain in the butt, and Leann was no doctor, but she knew the value of staying anesthetized.

One thing she knew she would never do is have kids, not after being around the little monsters like she had in this damn job. They were awful creatures, snot-nosed, smart-mouthed, loud, foolish . . . although she did take pride in her reputation among them. While she made herself scarce around teachers and Mrs. Evans, keeping encounters to a minimum and then behaving in a polite, respectful fashion, she relished the fear she instilled in the brats.

She knew they talked about her, and she loved it. She ruled these halls, secretly. When the teachers weren't around, those kids steered her a wide path, boy—and if some kid went crying or whining to the teachers about some mean thing she'd done, they got nowhere—the teachers only knew Miss Jones as unfailingly polite.

(Actually, the teachers thought of her as a lazy brownnoser, and suspected the kids who told on her were telling the truth; but nobody bothered doing anything about it, and unless or until a parent complained, nobody likely would.)

It was after four, with only a few lights on in the school, the last few teachers straggling out to the parking lot. Soon the building would be hers, to work in at her own speed, although *speed* was probably not an accurate word to describe the work methods of Leann Jones.

She was mopping the floor outside the third-grade classrooms, and the flop of the wet mop and the clanking bucket with its wringer were kind of noisy, which was maybe why she didn't notice the woman at first.

"*You* were bothering my daughter today."

Scared the hell out of Leann, the way the woman was just suddenly there, right in front of her, like a ghost that popped up.

A well-groomed, perfectly dressed ghost at that. Leann wondered what that dark blue dress must've cost, and those pearls. Everybody said Mrs. Sterling was beautiful, but to Leann, the woman looked witchy in the red glow of the EXIT sign nearby. She wasn't frowning, in fact she was faintly smiling, but Mrs. Sterling's eyes were fixed in a cold hard stare that unnerved Leann—not that she was about to show it.

Instead, Leann raised herself up and leaned on the mop handle and looked right at the rich bitch, sending a cold hard stare back at her. Who did she think she was messing with?

"I wasn't bothering nobody," Leann said. "You got permission to be in here after hours?"

"I'm a taxpayer," Mrs. Sterling said regally. "I don't need your permission."

"Well, you just get along about your business," the janitor said, and, having dismissed the snooty interloper, returned to her mopping.

But the woman remained planted there, frozen in place before Leann, saying, "What were you saying to my daughter today?"

Leann straightened and leaned on the mop handle again and smirked at her visitor. "You mean, that I seen you in there in Mrs. Withers's room? That I heard you two *talkin'* in there?"

The woman's eyes tightened; the left one

twitched. "Is that what you told the police?"

"I didn't tell the police *nothin'*!" Leann said indignantly.

When Mrs. Sterling replied, her face was a cold immobile mask, but a tremor of rage colored her voice. "I want you to stay away from my daughter."

"*And* the police?" Leann laughed, once, smirking. "Maybe I should go see 'em. Maybe I'd get a big ol' horselaugh out of a fine lady like you, puttin' up with all that bullshit. You'd make the papers, and not the society page this time!"

"I won't have you bothering her," Mrs. Sterling said softly, the tremor still underlining her words, "or embarrassing me."

Leann raised an eyebrow, smirked again. "Maybe you should make it worth my while . . ."

Footsteps echoed behind Leann—another teacher straggling out; she hunkered over her mop, getting back to work, while whoever it was walked by. Leann kept her back to Mrs. Sterling, making sure the teacher was out of sight, saying, "I know you didn't do nothin'. Fine lady like you. But maybe it'd be worth your while to—"

But Leann, turning back around now, found she was talking to nobody.

Just an empty hallway.

She looked every which way, but Mrs. Sterling was gone. Disappearing the same way she'd arrived: like a damn ghost. How'd she do that?

Unnerved now, well and truly spooked, Leann got back to work, in fact working more industriously than usual, because it helped get that weird woman off her mind. How did a cute kid like Jessica Ann Sterling wind up with a witch like that for a mom? There were, Leann decided, some pretty creepy people in this lousy world.

In her room, where she'd gone to get comfier, ponytailing her hair back, slipping into a sweater and jeans, Jessica Ann sat at her little desk and kept at her homework. She was distracted, however, and sat thumping the eraser end of her pencil on her geography paper while she looked up at the three gold Outstanding Student plaques. They nagged at her; they raised Lieutenant March's question.

If you should happen to find that plaque. . . .

Finally, she couldn't stand it anymore. She almost ran from her room, to her mommy's bedroom around the corner down the hall near the stairs.

Poised in the doorway, the child peeked in the room. The lights were off, except for one Mommy had forgotten to turn off, in the closet. She of course knew Mommy wasn't home and yet stepping inside Mommy's personal domain, without permission, was terrifying to her. Invading Mommy's privacy was one of the most unthinkable sins in a house where many such sins hung over every word and deed.

When she finally got the courage and stepped inside, it never occurred to her to turn on the light. Instead, she searched the room in the near dark, with only the light that edged from beneath the double door of the closet and seeped in from the hallway to guide her.

She looked in Mommy's nightstand drawer and caught a flash of something gold and shiny—but it was only a paper opener. The child held it up, and the sharp knifelike object seemed suddenly ominous. She tossed it back in the drawer, shoved the drawer shut. The nightstand had only one drawer, below it was an open display area, where Mommy had a small potted plant—but something gold and square was tucked alongside the plant. . . .

She snatched the square object out, and found herself holding a small ornamental gold-brass box. Sighing, she slid it back next to the plant.

Next she looked under the bed, practically crawling underneath it: nothing there, except two suitcases of Mommy's. She checked in those—not a thing.

Soon she found herself doing the unimaginable: opening the double doors of Mommy's closet, going through her things, bending to look among and behind the many pairs of fashionable shoes, rising to riffle through the hanging clothing, then stepping on tippy toes to get at the shelf above—where something gold and square glittered!

She snatched it down—and it was a purse.

A gold glitter purse. She shook her head and got back on tiptoes and returned it to its perch. Then she moved to the nearby highboy, again getting on her toes to check the big bowl atop the chest of drawers.

Empty.

Now the truly unthinkable: going through the drawers of Mommy's personal belongings; she did this quickly but thoroughly, and in the middle drawer, amid lingerie and lace and satin underthings that didn't seem like anything Mommy would wear at all, the child found something, something square and hard and wooden.

She withdrew it from the drawer and stood looking at the blank oblong minislab of wood, hoping that it was something other than what she knew it had to be. Desperately, she tried to think of other possibilities—a wall decoration, perhaps, or maybe a preserved diploma, or how about a wooden tablet with a saying on it, like THERE'S NO PLACE LIKE HOME. Turning it slowly in her hands, wanting to flip it instantly but not daring, putting herself through excruciating suspense in trade for a few more seconds of not knowing an awful truth, she was suddenly caught in the glow of the plaque's gold-metal face . . .

. . . OUTSTANDING STUDENT OF THE YEAR . . .

. . . and her fingers flew off it as if it were a burner on a hot stove, and she dropped it and barely heard the *thunk* as she ran out of the room, leaving it there in the middle of the carpet, the highboy drawer open, closet doors wide open, her mind unable to grasp anything but the all-pervasive horror of a knowledge that had changed Jessica Ann Sterling forever.

*   *   *

When the lights went out, Leann Jones froze, bent over with mop in hand, startled as hell. But that only lasted a moment. This wasn't the first time a damn fuse had blown in this worn-out, rundown excuse for a school.

Cursing the fuse, she slammed her mop handle against a locker, found her way to her nearby janitorial supply cart, and plucked her long-handled flashlight from its slot.

Of course, it might not be a fuse. It might be those little assholes again. On two occasions, some unknown brat or brats who'd hidden in the school after dismissal, waiting for the right moment, had yanked down the master breaker switch, just as a practical joke, to plunge McKinley into darkness and make a little trouble for their nemesis, Miss Jones.

Even as she cursed them, she had to smile a little. It was a compliment, in a way, an affirmation of her importance in their petty little lives, for them to plot such elaborate revenge.

Her flashlight's beam cutting through the pitch black, Leann was moving around the corner when she practically bumped into Mrs. Jensen.

Both women reacted as if the other had said "Boo," scaring the respective bejesus out of each other, and both women worked quickly to recover their dignity, Mrs. Jensen saying, "Better get those lights fixed."

And Leann, as soon as the assistant principal was out of earshot, muttered to herself, "No shit, Sherlock," and rounded the corner and headed to the door to the furnace room.

Though she'd been in there many times, the furnace room wasn't really a work area of Leann's, and in the utter darkness, relieved only by the searching beam of the flashlight, she felt completely disoriented. A noise at her left attracted her attention—metal rattling—and she threw the flashlight beam that way. *Are those damn kids in here?*

But her flashlight saw only cement walls and the open pipes that snaked up and down and around, and then a shape caught her eye. *Was that somebody?* No—a ladder against the wall.

She knew the fuse box was behind the twin furnaces, and around to the left . . . or was it the right? Her flashlight got her to the pathway between the blocky furnaces, and she moved between them, only to have a stray blast of steam scare the hell out of her. She paused, got her breath, and tried to get her bearings—to the left, right?

She moved along slowly, trying not to bump into a low-riding pipe or a sudden support beam, and then there it was: that big nasty fuse box that hadn't been updated since the school was built . . . with its main breaker switch down, in the OFF position.

A smile tickled her lips; it *was* those damn kids. . . .

She sauntered up to the box, a huge wall-mounted affair almost as big as she was, shook her head and laughed, and threw the switch back into the up, ON, position. The lights came on all over the school . . .

though just one fairly dim one switched back on in here.

Hand still on the switch, she leaned her weight on it, smirking, wondering if she could figure out which kids had done this so she could make their little lives miserable.

That was when a huge splash of water came from behind and drenched her, head to toe.

Astounded, enraged, soaked, she whirled, but before she could see who had done this or say a single word, from the shadows came the object that had contained the liquid she now wore: a bucket, her bucket, empty now, hurled at her, landing in her arms, and she reflexively clutched the metal pail even as its weight and the power with which it was pitched sent her backward, her balance off just enough for her to fall against the fuse box, her soaked, dripping metal-clutching body igniting an explosive torrent of electrical shock that in five seconds of hell paralyzed her and fried her, putting out the building's lights again, and hers, boiling her brain, disrupting the electrical circuit in her heart, stopping its beat, killing her very dead in a lovely Fourth of July–like shower of sparks.

The dead woman dropped the bucket, fell to her knees, and then, like the slab of cooked meat she'd become, flopped onto her side. Her eyes bulged a little more than usual, but at least they hadn't popped, as they well might have from the several thousand volts that passed through a body from which smoke now rose like ground fog. Those eyes, which someone who loved her had once found beautiful, did not see the high heels and sleekly ny-loned legs of the woman who emerged from the shadows to stroll casually by, just checking to see if Miss Jones would be tormenting children any longer.

When the woman, satisfied, moved on, one lone tear trickled down from one dead eye of Leann Jones, but no one saw it, except for the cyclops eye of the flashlight the janitor had dropped, which was filling her lifeless face with its beam.

Finally rational thought broke through the horror clutching her mind, and Jessica Ann remembered the condition in which she'd left her mother's room.

Quickly, she moved back into the bedroom, still not turning on the light, closing the closet doors, picking up the plaque, noting the obvious finger-prints on its gold face, using a sheer pair of pink satin panties to buff it clean, returning the plaque to her mother's drawer, to its hiding place buried under the lacy underthings, closing the drawer, and leaving. Quickly.

Back on her bed, she clutched her teddy bear to her, its wide button eyes no wider than hers.

Her mind was filled with awful thoughts. Had Mr. Sterling really died of a heart attack? What really happened that afternoon Mommy and Daddy went boating?

"Jessica Ann!"

The sound of her mother's voice gave her a jolt.

She jerked toward the doorway, where Mommy was leaning in, with the loveliest smile.

"Oh, I didn't mean to startle you, honey," she said. "Sorry I took so long." She stepped inside, holding something behind her. "I ran into an old friend at the store. We talked and talked."

Whenever her mother sounded this "nice," it made Jessica Ann suspicious, but right now the girl was too numb to wonder what Mommy had really been up to.

"Ready for Chinese," her mother asked, revealing a carryout package in either hand, balancing like little scales from their metal handles, "and a movie?"

"Great," Jessica Ann managed, but she couldn't quite muster a smile to go with it.

Chapter Eleven

Her mother dropped her off at school, barely before the bell rang. Jessica Ann usually took the bus, but she'd almost stayed home that morning, saying she felt sick, when really she was just exhausted from a nearly sleepless night.

"You don't have a temperature," Mommy said, feeling the forehead of the child sitting up in bed. "Don't you have a big test today?"

"Yes. In science."

"Did you prepare for it?"

Jessica Ann nodded.

"You wouldn't stay home to get out of it? You wouldn't lie to your mother?"

Jessica Ann shook her head, no.

"Well," Mommy said, "why don't you stay here in bed and rest, and I'll check back in a few minutes, and we'll see how you feel." Mommy patted the girl's blanket-covered leg. "Don't worry about missing your bus. I'll run you."

"Okay, Mommy."

Lying in bed, with the sun streaming in around the shade, didn't prove restful, her mind beginning to swim with the dark thoughts that had kept her up most of the night.

So ultimately Jessica Ann had decided to go to school, and when at the last moment she entered class, she found the room buzzing with whispered conversation. At first she dismissed the grapevine gibber as her classmates taking advantage of the substitute teacher—and Miss Morrison, who looked distracted and troubled, wasn't doing anything to quiet them.

In her immaculate navy dress with white Peter Pan collar and plaid bow, her hair ponytailed with a matching bow, Jessica Ann sat quietly going over the science chapter she would be tested upon, a perfect young lady in a storm of restless kids. Before long, Jessica Ann began to realize that something was up—that the chatter around her dealt with one subject, with one rumor that was being passed around and elaborated upon, though she had no idea what that rumor was. No one told her, and sitting in front as she was, if she were to turn and ask, she'd be flaunting bad behavior right in front of Miss Morrison.

And no one leaned in to share the rumor with her. She did have a few friends in class, and was well-liked and even admired. (She would have found it impossible to believe, but her peers considered her "popular," because she was, after all, pretty and smart and nice, most of them keeping a strangely respectful distance, as if she were classroom royalty.) But Jessica Ann had no really close friends—Mommy didn't like her to go to other kids' houses, and whenever kids came over to Jessica Ann's, they found the house rules too oppressive, the snacks too stingy, the recreational activities too limited.

So Jessica Ann had no idea what had been going around McKinley quicker than the flu, had no idea that the hottest rumor in the history of the school had blazed across the playground before she got there, a wild rumor that would soon become legendary at McKinley because it was that rare wild rumor that happened to be true.

Mrs. Evans appeared at the doorway—not a good sign. Miss Morrison walked over to meet the principal, and they spoke briefly, and then the two women walked into the classroom and positioned themselves before the students, Miss Morrison off to one side, the pastel colors of the wall map behind her contrasting with her gray suit; the substitute teacher looked very professional today—and distraught.

If Miss Morrison looked distraught, Mrs. Evans looked downright devastated. Her kind features drooped with the weight of some terrible concern, and Jessica Ann began to feel her heart race. What now? Wasn't Mrs. Withers dying enough?

What was this rumor that had her classmates in an uproar?

Whatever it was, that uproar—and the presence of Mrs. Evans—finally snapped Miss Morrison into action.

"Class, Mrs. Evans has something important to tell you," she said in a loud firm voice. "Class, *please!*"

And hearing docile Miss Morrison bark at them shut thirty little traps instantly. Actually, twenty-nine, because Jessica Ann's wasn't open. Her eyes were, however, and very wide, as she took in with horror the announcement her principal had to make.

"People," Mrs. Evans said, hands clasped before her, her dark blue blouse and gray slacks appropriate to her somber demeanor, "I'm sorry to have to tell you that we've had another tragedy here at McKinley."

A murmur of reaction passed across the classroom.

"Our janitor . . ." Mrs. Evans spoke the two words in a loud manner that hushed the murmur, then lowered her voice, gravely. ". . . died last night, in an unfortunate accident."

Behind Jessica Ann, Nate Allen, a gleeful kid in glasses and a soup-bowl haircut, leaned across the aisle to torment Lucy Peters.

"See, I *told* ya," he stage-whispered. "She got *fried!*"

"Quiet!" Miss Morrison thundered.

Stunned by the slap of a word, the boy sank low in his seat, and a funereal silence settled over the room, hanging there for hours, like a storm cloud that never quite turned into rain.

Somehow she got through the day, science test included, but the dark thoughts of the night before had darkened further, and to the myriad emotions churning within her—fear, worry, suspicion, anxiety—was added another: guilt.

It was *her* fault, wasn't it? She had told Mommy about what Miss Jones said in the hallway yesterday—and now Miss Jones was dead.

Mrs. Evans had told the class this morning that she was arranging for counselors to help any of the children at school who might be troubled by what had happened lately at McKinley. If Jessica Ann told the counselors that her mommy had maybe killed her daddy, and Mr. Sterling, for their money, she wondered what advice they would have.

But she didn't ask them, or anybody. On the way to the gym after school, to line up for buses, she saw Mrs. Evans talking to the policeman, that detective, Lieutenant March.

". . . dropping like flies around here," he was saying, "you gotta admit . . ."

Mrs. Evans was shaking her head, and looked very sad.

Jessica Ann lowered her eyes and just walked along, trying to get lost in the chattering crowd, but Lieutenant March spotted her, and called out to her.

"Jessica Ann!"

And she stopped in her tracks as other kids moved and weaved around her.

"Do you have anything to tell me?" he asked.

His expression was both searching and sympathetic.

Should she tell him about what she'd been thinking? What if she was wrong about Mommy? What if she was *right*?

No matter what, Jessica Ann thought, *she's still my mommy. . . .*

"No, sir," Jessica Ann said, avoiding his eyes.

And she moved on, but her thoughts stayed on the same subject, even as Lieutenant March's eyes trailed after her.

She thought about Daddy, and Mr. Sterling . . . and then she thought about someone else she cared about.

And, throughout the next week, a week that found some of her fears subsiding into what seemed like a regular routine, she carried out a sort of campaign designed to protect that "someone" . . . and herself.

The next Friday evening, after supper, Mark was waiting at the bottom of the stairs when Mommy came down for that benefit dance they were going to. Sharing the easy chair near the entryway with Aunt Beth, where they were looking over the TV section of the paper together, Jessica Ann glanced sideways and up at the stairs, seeing first Mommy's shapely legs in dark nylons and black heels—then, there her mother was, looking like a movie star making a grand entrance in her short black cocktail dress with its rhinestone-accented sweetheart bodice and mesh top and sleeves.

Anticipating her arrival, Mark plucked Mommy's purse from the divider the phone sat on, and as she reached the bottom of the stairs, gave his date a bow, handing her the purse as if bestowing an award. She took it, smiled, and laughed gently at his tongue-in-cheek courtliness, and reached out to smooth and straighten the jacket of his dark suit, in a gesture that was both affectionate and possessive.

"Well," Mommy said, "we shouldn't be any later than . . ." She looked at Mark. ". . . midnight?"

He checked his watch and nodded.

Aunt Beth, with Jessica Ann cuddled next to her in the chair, looked up pleasantly and said, "Stay out as long as you like. Enjoy yourselves."

"You are so sweet to do this, Beth," Mommy said. "I owe you one."

"I stopped keeping track a long time ago," Aunt Beth said with a smirk, which was kind of a catty response coming from Aunt Beth, but Mommy didn't seem to mind, or anyway, notice.

Mark opened the door for Mommy, who seemed to be floating on air tonight, and he glanced over at Jessica Ann, who felt his gaze on her but did not acknowledge him with hers.

" 'Bye, angel!" he called from the doorway, smiling.

Again, Jessica Ann didn't look at him, just mumbled, " 'Bye," almost sullenly.

The child didn't see Mark's troubled expression as

he studied her for a few moments, before following her mother out.

Only then did Jessica Ann turn to look toward the door; her unhappy expression caught her aunt's attention.

"Is something wrong, Jessy?"

"No," Jessica Ann said, returning her attention to the TV section. "Nothing."

"You do know, don't you," Aunt Beth said, brushing a bang away from the girl's slightly furrowed forehead, "that there's nothing you can't talk to me about. . . ."

But Jessica Ann's attention was fixed on the TV listings.

"Is it what happened at school last week?" Aunt Beth probed, gently. "Your teacher . . . that janitor . . . ?"

"Oh!" Jessica Ann checked the time on her aunt's wristwatch, then looked up brightly at Beth. "Can we watch *Seinfeld?* Mommy doesn't like comedies, but I do."

Aunt Beth beamed at the child, and cuddled her close. "Sure, honey."

"Where's the remote? It's just starting. . . ."

The Hotel Carver, with its scenic view of the Mississippi River, ashimmer tonight with silver moonlight, was one of Ferndale's showplaces; a local industrialist with a love for his native city had made the turn-of-the-century hotel his personal project, renovating the six-story structure, restoring its rich woodwork, filling it with exquisite Victorian furnishings. The hotel's parking lot, tonight, was rife with BMWs, Cadillacs, Lincolns, and an occasional Jaguar or Porsche, like Mark's. The city's elite were in attendance, mingling with a number of local educators, at this benefit for the state chapter of the Literacy Volunteers of America. Mrs. Sterling didn't seem to notice the whispers among a cluster of teachers from McKinley when she and Mark passed by—though he did.

The same three-piece combo who'd been playing at the country club the night they met was playing a dreamy instrumental as Mark led his lovely date out onto the dance floor. In her simple black dress, with its glittering trim, the shapely little woman blew the competition—some of it years younger than her—easily away; that dazzling smile was underscored by a graceful almost girlish laugh he'd not heard from her before. Mark felt almost dizzy with her beauty.

But Mark had something else on his mind, and in the embrace of their slow dancing, her hand entwined with his over his heart, he drew away enough to ask, "Have you noticed anything . . . well, odd about Jessica Ann lately?"

She looked up at him, smiled, shrugged. "Not really."

"*I* have. . . . For the last week or so, she's been avoiding me . . . *snubbing* me, even."

"Oh," she said with a gently dismissive laugh, as

they drifted about the dance floor, "I never noticed that . . ."

He looked at her just sharply enough to let her know his concern was serious. "You don't think she's been kind of . . . moody?"

She shrugged a little. "Well, maybe she's jealous."

Mark had to laugh. "What does that mean?"

Now her smile turned teasing, yet remained affectionate. "I think she's got a little-girl crush on you, mister."

"No. Really?"

She nodded. "What's been added around the Sterling house, this last 'week or so'?"

And now it came to him. He threw his head back, feeling stupid, then began to nod as she continued.

She joined in with his nodding. "You've begun staying over occasionally . . . right?"

"Right. Right. . . ."

She enfolded herself back into his arms and patted his shoulder tenderly; she couldn't see her lover's face tighten into something troubled.

They sat at a tiny table for two, preferring each other's company over any others', and when Mrs. Sterling excused herself to powder her nose, Mark rose and moved through the crowd, nodding to some of the new friends he had made over the last several months, as he headed for the men's room.

In the little bathroom, he stood at the first of two urinals, unzipping, lost in concerned thought, conscious of someone else at the urinal next to him—someone slumped over rather drunkenly, leaning against the porcelain top with a drink resting there—but not really paying any attention to who it was. Urinal etiquette required a straight-ahead stare.

"Don't be surprised to see me here," Lieutenant March said, looking up with drink-hooded eyes. "This is where all the dicks hang out."

Mark, startled at first, scowled at the cop. "Are you out of your mind, March, talking to me here?"

"Why? We're not gonna run into Mrs. Sterling . . ." And March looked over at him lecherously. "Not unless you two kids have somethin' *kinky* in mind. . . ."

The cop was slurring his words and his eyes were cloudy.

"I go to all these charity balls," March said, zipping up with some difficulty, weaving away from the urinal. "What can I tell you? My wife is loaded. . . ."

"Yeah, well so are you," Mark said, zipping up, turning to confront the cop, who was slumped over the sink, washing up. "Look, I don't know any more today than I did yesterday, and you are going to blow my damn cover, if you keep this up."

March looked up in the mirror over the sink and made eye contact with Mark, standing behind him.

"This is a woman," March said, holding up two fingers, "who killed two people in two days."

"We don't *know* that for sure."

March wheeled and suddenly he seemed more steady. "Don't we, Mr. Consolidated Life? What . . . the longer you stay on the job, the bigger the paycheck? Or is little Mommy just a good lay?"

Mark grabbed the cop by his lapels, but it was March who spoke. "Get your hands off me. Get them off—*now*."

And on that final word, the cop brushed Mark's hands off him with one surprisingly powerful hand.

Mark tried to compose himself. Breathing hard, trying to reign in his anger, he said, "Listen, I do not work for you—" Mark shook his head; why even try to reason with this madman? "Just stay away. *If* I get anything—"

"Oh, I already know you're gettin' somethin'," March said, chuckling, wearing that lecherous look again, but the look immediately darkened and March's eyes were tight and forbidding. "But you know what I wonder . . . I wonder if you know what kind of game you're playing . . . and who you're playing it with?"

Mark took the words like a punishment he had to suffer, absorbed them, then sighed and held up his hands as if to keep from laying them on March again.

"I'm outta here. Stay the hell away."

As Mark was moving to the door, March said, "Damn it, there's a little child involved—"

Mark wanted to hear no more. He went out into the ballroom and caught up with his date, and soon they were locked in each other's embrace, swaying about the dance floor. Seeing March carrying a cocktail to his lovely blond wife at the bar made Mark uneasy; like many undercover operators, Mark was most comfortable in the false life he was leading, and the reminder of reality unnerved him, particularly with the questions that the reality of this situation raised. Was this lovely woman, this bundle of soft curves in his arms, this sensual lover, this conscientious mother, the monster March thought her to be?

The monster Mark had been sent here to prove she was?

But when he saw the dreamy, romantic expression on her face, as she nestled herself amorously into his shoulder, her platinum hair tickling him, her perfume (the Red Door he'd bought her) intoxicating him, he could not quite yet convince himself of her guilt.

He was lying to himself, of course, but then, he was good at lying, and damn good at determining the guilt of others, if not facing his own.

Chapter Twelve

The woman slumbering next to him was an appealing combination of innocence and worldliness. A cool spring breeze whispered through an open window, rustling sheer curtains, and the sheet and comforter were pulled down well below their waists, the air soothing on his bare chest where the unbuttoned pajama top lay open. She lay on her back, but with her finely chiseled features facing him, her platinum hair barely mussed from sleep, the trim yet rounded figure ensconced in a short lacy midnight-blue nightie, the firm fullness of her bosom kindling memories of the sensual, animalistic passions this bedroom had seen, tonight included—deeply emotional responses from a woman who chose to present a cold, controlled image to the outer world. In repose, her face had a gentleness, a childlike quality that brought out her resemblance to her daughter; when the mind within that pretty head was in charge, however, all gentleness, anything childlike, was quite absent from her face.

Though tonight, at the charity dance, she had been radiant, animated, and, in her uncharacteristic happiness, giddy as a young girl. This response had warmed Mark at first, and then disturbed him; the bathroom encounter with March had spoiled a pleasant evening, and now—hours later, in the middle of the night—he was wide awake and staring, staring at a ceiling he couldn't quite make out in the darkness, staring into a situation that was teeming with temptations (most of which he'd already given in to) and complications.

The woman in bed beside him was probably a murderer. He hadn't gathered enough evidence to prove that, but March was right—she probably had killed any number of people. Still, he found her enormously attractive, and the pleasures of her bed were considerable.

The real problem was the other two females entangled in this woman's web. Mark had come to be very fond of Beth, who in her way was as lovely as her sister, and who was obviously attracted to him (she was the one temptation in this case he had thus far resisted). But mostly it was Jessica Ann who had his heart tied in a knot. He had come to love that little girl with a purity he didn't know he was still capable of. In a terrible world, a cynical hellhole that counted him a card-carrying member, Mark had seen redemption in the simple innocence of this child, an innocence remarkably echoed in the slumbering face of her beautiful mother.

His beeper sounded, startling him, and irritating him, and he bounded from bed, fumbled with his trousers on a chair on the other side of the nightstand, shutting it off, watching the woman in bed to see if she'd been roused or wakened.

Apparently not.

He sighed with relief, then put the beeper back and slipped out of the bedroom, padding down the stairs in his pajamas, to the phone on the divider between entryway and living room. He punched in the numbers and waited for it to connect.

He got the Consolidated Life switchboard recording and waited for the opportunity to punch in the extension of his supervisor, Clemens, who answered at once.

"Little late for you to be working, isn't it?" Mark whispered tightly, putting some false cordiality into his voice.

"No rest for the wicked. So what's—"

"What in the hell is wrong with you?" Mark demanded, working to keep his voice down despite the rage welling up. "Has everybody gone crazy on this thing? *Never* beep me at night . . . I swear I'll take a hammer to the . . . beeping thing. . . ."

"It's been a week since we heard 'boo' out of you, buddy. Figured I oughta catch you when nobody was around . . ."

"The way this thing is heating up, you don't contact me at all—you can get word to me through that cop."

"Why can't—"

"Because I'm spending too much time with her, now—and you'll blow my cover!"

And he set the phone down, almost a slam, a little too loud maybe, and turned to look up toward the railing in front of the bedroom, to make sure he didn't have company—and caught sight not of the mother, but—damn!—the *daughter*, down on her knees listening, peering down through the rails like she was a prisoner behind bars, scurrying away like a little mouse, probably thinking he hadn't seen her.

But he had.

What had she heard?

This time he said it aloud, slumping against the post of the divider: "Damn."

He went up the stairs, took the jog in the hallway around to her room, where a sliver of light under her door beckoned. He should have thought of that—earlier this week, he'd noticed that light on very late at night, when he got up to answer nature's call; he had asked the child, next morning, what she was doing up that late and she had said only, in the sullen manner she'd been subjecting him to lately, "Reading."

He knocked gently on her door, and her voice came, in tentative response: "Yes?"

He cracked the door open, peeked in. She was under the green comforter, sitting up in bed, a book folded open on her nightstand, where the lamp was on, and she was fiddling with a little kelly-green outfit her teddy bear was wearing. She didn't look at him.

"Did I wake you, angel?"

"No."

"Can I come in for a second?"

"Okay," she said noncommittally, shrugging a little, still not acknowledging him with even a glance.

He stepped inside, shut the door, buttoning his pajama top as he approached the child's bed. He sat at the far end, keeping a discreet distance from her.

"Angel . . . what is it?"

Now she looked at him, but with a blank indifference in her big blue eyes, her emotions hiding behind a cold mask; she'd had a good teacher, after all. "What's what?"

He leaned in a little. "What's *wrong?*"

Now her expression mixed bewilderment with impatience, a childhood specialty. "Nothing."

"You've barely spoken to me for days. . . ."

She shrugged and looked away.

"You know you're number one on my personal chart, don't you?" he asked, leaning in closer.

Her body rustled under the covers as she withdrew from him.

"I dunno," she mumbled, pointedly keeping her gaze directed away from his.

He kept trying. "Is it something I said? Is it something I did? Is it because . . . I've been sleeping over?"

She said nothing, eyes still looking past him.

"Don't you think I'd make a good daddy?"

And now she shifted her body beneath the covers, turning away from him, toward her nightstand, where her gaze fell upon the framed photo of her father, and the cold mask melted and she lurched forward, taking the comforter with her, hugging Mark, clutching Mark, desperately, sobbing.

"Angel," he said, patting her back, there there, there there.

"I . . . I wanted to chase you away. . . ."

Astounded, he eased her out of the hug, yet held onto her arms as he peered into her beautiful tear-streaked face. "You wanted to chase me away? Why on earth—"

"Because . . ." And she glanced at her daddy's picture, then back at Mark. ". . . because you *would* make a good daddy . . ." Tiny voice breaking, love luminous in her tear-shiny eyes. ". . . and I don't want you to die. . . ."

Was there a more sensitive child on the planet, he wondered, or a bigger heel than himself? He patted her hand as she scooched beside him.

"I'm . . . I'm having bad thoughts." She seemed embarrassed, and guilty, about it.

Watching her carefully, holding her by the arms gently but firmly, he asked, "What bad thoughts, angel?"

"That Mommy killed Miss Jones," she blurted, as if confessing her own crimes, "and Mrs. Withers . . . and maybe even Mr. Sterling . . . and Daddy. For their money . . ." And now she winced with the emotional pain. ". . . and *you* have money, too. . . ."

She gazed at him with a love so pure, his heart leapt, and sank, and she began to sob. He knew he should just take her in his arms and comfort her, tell her her worries were unfounded, soothe her with lies about her mommy being innocent. That was the right thing to do.

But he was in his way like March, a detective, a cop, and he found himself glancing at the door, making sure it was shut nice and tight, and now he looked at the girl with a level gaze and a firm, hard expression.

He had a job to do.

"How grown up can you be, Jessica Ann?"

"I don't know," she said through her tears. "Real grown-up, I hope, if I have to."

"Good," he said, smiling tightly. "Because I want to level with you about something. Something that might make you mad at me. . . ."

The eyes widened with surprise and froze, while the chin quivered with sobs that were beginning to subside.

"Why, Mark?"

"You heard me talking downstairs, didn't you, Jessica Ann . . . on the phone?"

Now she seemed a little ashamed, knowing she'd been caught at her eavesdropping, but she fessed up with a nod.

"Did you hear what I was saying?"

"Kind of."

"Did you understand the conversation?"

"I'm . . . I'm not sure."

"You see, I haven't been completely honest with you, Jessica Ann . . ." He could no longer meet her clear gaze, and he hung his head. ". . . in fact, I've lied."

Now the eyes went very wide. "What?"

He sighed, forced himself to look right at her. "My real name is Mark, but it's not Mark Jeffries. I'm what's called a private investigator. . . . I'm working for an insurance company, the company looking into Mr. Sterling's death. . . ."

And now she drew away, rustling the covers in indignation, in outrage, in shock, pulling the comforter up and around her, as if to hide beneath it, but then leaning forward slightly, the eyes suddenly narrowing, appraising him with a startlingly adult wariness.

"But you and Mommy . . ."

He dropped his gaze again, then forced himself to look at her. "That wasn't . . . wasn't very nice, but it wasn't part of any plan, Jessica Ann. It just sort of . . . happened."

"Do you love her?"

He swallowed. "Well, your mommy's a very beautiful woman, and charming . . ."

"Do you *love* her?"

The honesty of her gaze defeated him; he couldn't lie to her. He could barely get it out, his voice a whisper, breaking with emotion that surprised him.

"No."

She drew away again, folding her arms, protecting herself, weeping soundlessly, not looking at him, wanting no comfort, not wanting him in her life at all.

He shook his head, sighed, tried again. "Jessica Ann, what I did wasn't very nice, but I had to get close to your mommy—"

"You sure did!" She looked away, chin quivering.

"I had to get the truth." He edged closer. "Jessica Ann, I think your mommy is a murderer . . ."

Judging by the child's shifting eyes, it was clear she held the same suspicion.

". . . and with your help—"

Now she looked at him again, amazed and incensed. "*My* help?"

He tried to keep his voice calm, reasonable. "Actually, it's your mommy who needs the help. If she's doing these things . . . and we both think she is . . . then she's a sick person, and she needs to be stopped, and she needs to be helped."

"Helped," Jessica Ann said, nodding.

Was he beginning to get through to her?

Encouraged by this positive response, he leaned forward, saying, "If you could just think back, and tell me about some of the things you've seen, then we might be able to—"

But that was as far as he got.

Because the door flew open, slapping the wall like a spurned suitor, rattling toys and possessions and handles on drawers; even the plaques over Jessica Ann's desk threatened to jump off their nails.

And she floated in like a ghost, an apparition in a

tightly belted hunter-green robe, hands behind her, face beautiful, immobile, emotionless, though something wild was in the wide eyes.

"Close your eyes, dear," the girl's mother said, almost sweetly.

And the child, who had fallen over on her teddy, as if the door opening had been a blow that knocked her aside, did as she was told.

And his lover smiled at him, just faintly, her eyes softening, yet conveying so much, telling him exactly what she was about to do, and he made no move to escape, not even to protect the child, because he knew the child was the one thing this woman would not harm, at least not right now, and he slumped ever so slightly, in surrender, in defeat, and was not in the least surprised when the gun came out from behind her back, and her face turned cold and hard as the metal of a revolver that fired once, knocking him back but not off the bed, tearing into his shoulder, and again, into his chest, sending him backward, flecks of his blood kissing the screaming child's cheek, kissing her good-bye, the ringing of gunfire in his ears turning off as if by a switch, as he stared at the ceiling of a bedroom once again, this time seeing nothing at all, not even darkness.

Chapter Thirteen

Mark was sprawled on his back on the bed, hanging half-off it, arms in a posture of useless surrender, his pale blue pajamas stained scarlet in two terrible spots, his eyes full of surprise, but she knew he wasn't seeing anything. Jessica Ann knew he was dead, and so she stopped screaming, screaming would do no good now, and she leaned forward to help him, hoping she was wrong, and even if Mark was dead, her impulse was to hold him, to hug him, to wish him back to life; but her mother, setting down the gun on the nightstand by daddy's picture, was leaning in to stop her, to draw her away from the corpse that used to be Mark. The child began to sob, saying, "No" over and over again, until it became one long word, "Nononononono," that was not really a word at all, but the sound of shock and sorrow.

Mommy pushed teddy aside, drew back the covers, and gathered the child into her arms, saying, "Come on, sweetie, come on," shushing her gently, tugging the girl's little nightshirt down modestly, getting her on her feet.

Jessica Ann was still looking toward Mark, her sobs beginning to escalate, as Mommy said soothing words, quieting words. The flecks of blood had dripped together into a sort of crimson scar on the child's cheek, and the mother noticed this, saying, "Awww," and licking a finger, wiping away the blood, then licking the blood from the finger to wipe the rest away.

Then Mommy lifted Jessica Ann into her arms as if the eleven-year-old were a baby, and as her mother was carrying her away from the carnage of the bedroom, the child made one last desperate attempt to reach out to the man she would never call Daddy.

Her sobs eased as Mommy caressingly carried her down the stairway, and across the living room to the couch, where not long ago Jessica Ann and Mark had talked about everybody dying someday. Her mother held the girl, cradling her, snuggling her, rocking her.

The child, numb though she was, regressing into near infancy, allowed herself to be cuddled and comforted by the woman she'd just seen commit murder, because there was nowhere else to turn, was there? Part of the child detached, floated, looking objectively at her mother, noting that her mother seemed sad, a rare condition in Mommy's case. Maybe Mommy had really liked Mark; or maybe Mommy felt bad about Jessica Ann seeing her do what she did.

Still holding the child in her lap, Mommy withdrew a tissue from a pocket of her robe and dried her daughter's tears; and then she did the same for herself. She had wept, Mommy had wept, had cried, no question this time, not like at Mr. Sterling's funeral.

The child just hoped her mommy wasn't sad because she was thinking of doing something bad to Jessica Ann, too.

"We have to call the police now, dear," Mommy said reasonably, though there was an unfamiliar tremor of emotion in the well-modulated, musical voice.

Jessica Ann glanced up. "Yes, Mommy."

"And when they come," Mommy said, "we have to stick together."

Mommy brought the child's face up to hers, firmly but gently, a flower plucked, its petals intact, lifted for its fragrance; she held the child's face delicately in her palms, compelling the child to look at her. "Do you understand, dear?"

She winced in confusion. "I'm not sure . . ."

"We have to tell them things that fit together—like a *puzzle* fits together." Mommy cupped Jessica Ann's chin and looked at the girl, her smile tender, her eyes searching. "Do you understand, dear?"

"Y-yes, Mommy."

Mommy drew the child close to her, resting Jessica Ann's head on her shoulder, stroking her hair gently. Jessica Ann closed her eyes, nestling against Mommy's nubby robe, cherishing the warmth of Mommy's embrace, the loving timbre of her voice, achieving at long last a deep emotional togetherness with her mother, receiving in these dreadful moments something the child had long craved. It was the highlight of Jessica Ann's young life, and the low point.

"Mark did . . ." And she spat out the next word like a bitter seed. ". . . *bad* things to Mommy tonight." Hurt mingled with indignation in her tone. "Bedroom things . . . that I didn't want him to do."

She was stroking the child's shoulder, at first soothingly, but now nervously, and Jessica Ann was surprised by the feelings Mommy's voice revealed. Mommy looked at her piercingly. "You do understand, dear . . . ?"

"I . . . I think so."

"And when Mommy heard Mark in your bedroom . . ." Her eyes traveled upward, as if she were trying to look through the ceiling at where it happened. ". . . she was afraid he might be doing those same bad things to you."

Jessica Ann drew back from her mother's embrace, to look at her; the child shook her head and conveyed with her steady gaze the truth of her words: "But . . . he didn't."

"That doesn't matter," Mommy said firmly, then her voice softened, though she held a lecturing finger up to the girl's face. "And you don't have to say he did, either."

"I'm glad, Mommy."

Mommy's smile was lovely, and loving. "I wouldn't want you to lie."

"No, Mommy."

Mommy drew her daughter close to her again, nestled her back in the hollow of her shoulder, stroking the girl's neck, smoothing her hair, gazing upward, head high. "And those things Mark told you—about being an investigator for an insurance company? *Forget* them. He never said those things."

"Oh," Jessica Ann said. "Okay, Mommy."

And now Mommy held her child before her again, and looked right in the girl's eyes. "Because if you tell . . ."

Suddenly the mother seemed very young to her little girl, pulling herself down below the child, looking up at her, making a parent of the child for a moment, placing the mother's destiny in the hands of the child.

". . . it would get Mommy in a lot of trouble. And we don't want that, do we?"

And the child, shaking her head, said, "No, Mommy."

Then, as if each was looking into the mirror of the other, they saw an expression of unconditional love, of tears held back, that was the closest moment they'd ever shared.

The woman drew her child to her breast and in a voice trembling with emotion rare for her, in a state other than rage that is, said, "Who's your best friend?"

Jessica Ann swallowed, smiled the tightest, saddest, happiest of smiles. "You are, Mommy. . . ."

Mommy daintily took Jessica Ann's hand and held it within hers, as if it were her most precious possession, and clasped it against her heart.

"Who loves you more than *anything* on God's green earth. . . ."

Nodding with certainty, the child sobbed, "You do, Mommy."

Beaming through tears, nodding with satisfaction, Mommy stroked Jessica Ann's head. "Good girl."

Mommy held her there for a short while, then patted her shoulder, and eased the child onto the couch, helping her recline there, smoothing her nightshirt, saying, "Here, baby . . . here, baby. . . ."

Then Mommy rose, holding a finger to her lips, signaling the child to stay quiet, and went quickly, efficiently, to the phone on the divider. Entirely self-composed now, with a deadly calm, she punched in 911 and waited patiently.

Then Jessica Ann watched as her mother exploded into an emotional, tearful, barely controlled hysteria: "Please, help! Please hurry! We need an ambulance . . . he was molesting my *daughter!*"

Sighing, shaking her head, rolling her eyes, thinking, *There she goes again*, the girl turned over on the couch, her back to her mother now, who was practically screaming into the phone, "Yes, I shot him! *Shot* him!"

Chapter Fourteen

There were vehicles with flashing lights outside the house—a fire department rescue truck, police cars, an ambulance—and a lot of men and women inside the house, throughout the night, some of them police, some of them in uniform, some in regular clothes, some using cameras.

At first Lieutenant March questioned Mommy in the kitchen, while Jessica Ann and Aunt Beth, in sweatshirt and exercise pants, sat together in that chair by the phone on the divider, near the front door, where they'd been sitting the last time Mark left the house. Two ambulance attendants—the same ones who'd taken Mrs. Withers away—were wheeling out their stretcher, with Mark on it, his body covered by a white sheet; he looked like a ghost. They had some trouble with the door, it was awkward for the one man to reach behind him, so Jessica Ann scampered from the chair and opened the door to help.

"Thanks, honey," the man said, and to his partner added, "Nice little girl."

Poised in the doorway now, Jessica Ann watched them wheel the stretcher out; when they carted the stretcher over the curb, Mark's arm fell out and his expensive watch glinted with the red flashing ambulance lights. Aunt Beth came up beside her in the doorway, put an arm around her shoulder, and just as the ambulance doors were being shut, taking Mark forever away, she closed the front door and walked Jessica Ann to the dining room table.

The child sat there while Lieutenant March continued his interrogation of her mother, which had moved to the living room now. Mommy sat in the regal chair near the couch, wearing her green robe, her arms folded tight to her, her expression as blank as a doll's.

Lieutenant March had told Jessica Ann she couldn't use her bedroom tonight—it was X'ed off with yellow and black crime scene tape—but that was all right with her. She didn't think she could sleep in there, anyway.

Jessica Ann, quiet, inert, was seated at the head of the dining room table.

Her aunt leaned in supportively. "You don't have to tell me if you don't want to."

"Nothing to tell," Jessica Ann said flatly. "Mommy

thought Mark was going to do something bad to me. So she protected me."

She could see her Mommy being questioned, Lieutenant March pacing, growling his questions, Mommy answering quietly, expressing grave concern at the "tragedy," hands folded in her lap, yet dignified, peaceful, and as self-contained as a sewing kit.

"How about some cocoa?" Aunt Beth asked her niece.

"Okay," Jessica Ann said unenthusiastically, then not wanting to hurt Aunt Beth's feelings, added, "Thanks."

After her cocoa, Jessica Ann put her head on her folded arms, like kids do when they take naps at their desks at school, but she wasn't sleeping. Really, she wasn't even that tired—but she didn't want to talk to anybody, and if they thought she was asleep, maybe they'd leave her alone.

With Lieutenant March questioning Mommy out in the living room, Jessica Ann couldn't hear what they were saying, most of the time.

But sometimes it was easy to hear, like when Lieutenant March shouted, "No, you're not under arrest, and yes, you should contact your lawyer."

Even with her head down, Jessica Ann could hear the policeman tromp out to the kitchen. Aunt Beth had been staying out here, giving coffee to whoever wanted it, and Lieutenant March was returning his empty cup.

Right now, her aunt was behind the counter,

washing out cups, serving anyone who wandered in. She asked, "More coffee, Lieutenant?"

"Thanks," he said, handing her the cup. He leaned back against the counter. He was wearing the same shirt as when he questioned Jessica Ann at school; also the same gun. "Your sister is quite a woman."

Aunt Beth, refilling his cup, said, "You don't believe her, do you?"

"Do you?"

"Of course I believe her," Aunt Beth said, mildly indignant. "She's my sister."

"Yeah," March said, taking a sip, "and Jeffrey Dahmer was somebody's brother."

"That was uncalled for," Aunt Beth said, aghast.

"I suppose so. It's been a long night." He turned to look across the counter at Jessica Ann, apparently asleep on her folded arms. "I'll talk to your niece in the morning."

"Thank you for that much, anyway."

March nodded, sipped some more coffee, then headed back toward the living room, pausing at the refrigerator. "Maybe she should stay with you tonight."

"That's not my decision," Aunt Beth said.

He looked at her, hard. "Maybe it should be," he said, then went back in the living room, where things were finishing up.

Aunt Beth looked across the counter at Jessica Ann and said, "You aren't really asleep, are you?"

She looked up. "No."

Aunt Beth came around quickly and knelt next to

the seated child, looking up at her earnestly. She spoke quietly, almost a whisper. "What you told me . . . is that what *really* happened, Jessica Ann?"

"Mommy thought Mark was going to do something bad to me," Jessica Ann recited. "So she protected me."

Aunt Beth touched the child's arm, squeezed affectionately. "You love your mommy, don't you?"

She nodded. "Yeah."

"I love her, too."

"I know."

"But you're afraid of her, aren't you?"

"Sure." She shrugged. "Every kid's afraid of their parents."

"Beth!"

Mommy's outburst startled them both; they sucked in a breath as they turned to her, standing suddenly in the archway from the dining room to the kitchen.

"Maybe you'd better go now, Beth."

Aunt Beth rose. She wet her lips. "Maybe I should take Jessica Ann tonight. . . ."

"You've already done more than enough," Mommy said as she approached them, moving between the child and her aunt.

Backing away, Aunt Beth said, "I can stay, if you like. . . ."

Mommy, standing next to Jessica Ann at the table, settled a protective hand on the child's shoulder. "We appreciate your concern. But we've been through a lot of tragedy together, Jessica Ann and

I." She smiled down warmly at her daughter, then she looked over pointedly at her sister. "And we will make it through tonight just fine. . . . Won't we, dear?"

And she stroked the child's golden hair affectionately, as one might a beloved pet.

Nodding up at her, wide-eyed, Jessica Ann said, "Yes, Mommy."

Beth tried to reason with her sister, but soon she was getting the bum's rush, as the child's mother walked her firmly to the door.

"You take the couch, I'll take the chair," her sister said to the girl, and then guided—actually pushed—Beth out the door. "It'll be just like camping out. . . ."

And the door shut.

Beth, stumbling, almost falling from her sister's less than gentle nudge, swore silently, throwing her hands up and down, mad more at herself than at her sister, who was, after all, her sister, and couldn't help herself.

She walked away from the house, her mind alive with Lieutenant March's words, and her own fears and concerns. . . . Was it irresponsible of her to leave that child in that house with that woman? Was Jessica Ann safe? Was Beth abandoning her?

The night was dark and, for May, cold. She crossed her arms, huddling in on herself for warmth if not comfort, thoughts buzzing. Trying to find the resolve to go knock on that door and face up to her sister and, thinking, finally, to hell with the consequences, Beth turned back—just as the lights went out.

The last police car was pulling away as, sighing in defeat, she turned to leave. Consumed with worry, wishing she were stronger, Beth gave in to the darkness of the night and let it envelop her.

Chapter Fifteen

She was good. The bad ones usually were. No one knew their way around an interrogation like a born liar. Still, March had to try. He sat hunkered in his chair at one end of the table, taking notes, while stoic Mrs. Sterling sat to his left, with her attorney, keen-eyed Neal Ekhardt, directly across from the detective.

Late afternoon sunlight knifed its way through the blinds, shards of light that made patterns on the table, dappling decorative ferns and lending a golden glow to the rich dark wood of this deposition room in the Ferndale courthouse. Detective Coderoni and a rep from the DA's office stood behind Mrs. Sterling, backs to a window, witnessing the process, while a female clerk of the court, out of the way somewhere behind March, recorded the interview on videotape.

"So you didn't know," March said, "the man you were sharing your bed with was investigating you?"

In her widow's-black suit, with its dressy gold buttons and tapered waist, she presented a businesslike facade, yet there was also an aura of grave glamour, the platinum arcs of her hair framing finely carved features as serene and enigmatic as the Sphinx.

"Absolutely not," she said with crisp indignation.

She sat with her hands folded before her, prayerlike, staring straight ahead, as if she were studying a painting in a museum, but keeping her opinion of the painting to herself.

"Did you *suspect*—"

"Hasn't that been established, Lieutenant?" Ekhardt leaned forward, shaking his head in exasperation. "How many times do we have to go over this ground?"

At sixty-three, Neal Ekhardt was both craggy and distinguished; he was also expensive, and—though criminal law was not his sole province (divorce was probably his true forte)—he was the area's attorney of choice for the guilty rich. A broad-shouldered side of beef in a Brooks Brothers suit and striped silk tie, his close-cropped white hair contrasting vividly with his Florida tan, Ekhardt had slits in his lantern-jawed face that stone-gray eyes peered from, eyes that had seen just about everything life had to offer, eyes that could twinkle with leprechaun amusement, eyes that could flare with fiery rage, eyes that could soften with genuine compassion, eyes that could (like right now) convey weary contempt.

"She's told you she didn't know he was investigating her," Ekhardt said. "What part of 'no' don't you understand?"

"I suppose it *has* been established," March admitted, shrugging a little, looking at the imperturbable woman. "But it's also been established that the men you sleep with kinda make a bad habit out of *dying* on you . . . don't they, Mrs. Sterling?"

Ekhardt's hand sliced the air, like a pissed off priest making a partial benediction. "That's inappropriate, Lieutenant—"

"*Conveniently* dying, that is."

Mrs. Sterling glanced briefly March's way, but said nothing, her imperial bearing unruffled; but Ekhardt leaned forward, his well-grooved face clenched like a fist.

"Lieutenant. . . ." Ekhardt said sternly, packing a wealth of warning into the one word.

March gazed amiably at the interviewee. "How much money did you inherit when your first husband died, Mrs. Sterling?"

She swiveled her gaze to meet his; it was like watching a cannon being moved into correct firing position.

"How much money did your wife inherit when her first husband died?" she asked witheringly. "And where were *you* at the time?"

Ekhardt smiled over at her, patted her hand,

pleased with this response; and March had to smile himself. Oh, she was good, all right.

The daughter was even better.

While Mrs. Sterling waited out in the hall, Jessica Ann sat where her mother had; in a black blazer with a white blouse and black buttons, golden hair beautifully coiffed, hands folded, she was a miniature of her mommy right down to the impassively lovely face.

And, of course, Ekhardt again took the seat opposite March, sitting forward, ready to pounce on any legal bone.

"Jessica Ann," March said, looking up from doodling on his pad, "did Mark Patterson . . . or Jeffries, as you knew him . . ."

She gazed at him with such openness, such innocence, he could hardly bear to ask the damn question.

But he did: ". . . did he ever make an advance toward you, of a . . . sexual nature?"

The child began to speak, but Ekhardt touched her arm gently, shaking his head, no.

"There really should be a representative from Child Welfare," the attorney said pointedly to March, "if you insist on—"

"I am just trying to confirm your client's story, okay?" March said to the attorney. Then he turned to the child again. "Now, I apologize for asking, Jessica Ann, but did he?"

"No," she said, shaking her head. "But Mommy thought so."

"Oh, really?" March glanced at Ekhardt, and back at the girl. "Why is that, Jessica Ann?"

Her eyes widened as she drew back, while offering a possible solution to this mystery, posed in the form of a question: "Because he was in my bedroom, in his pajamas, in the middle of the night?"

March closed his eyes, sighed. What could he say to that?

Ekhardt lifted his hands, palms up, smiled mildly, and pronounced, "I think that's quite enough. Good afternoon."

And the attorney rose, gesturing for the child to come with him; taking her hand, he escorted her from the chamber—they might have been a proud grandfather and his adored little granddaughter leaving after a church service.

Rubbing a hand through his hair in frustration, March sat and looked bleakly down at the pad he'd been doodling on, knowing that doodling was about all he'd gotten for his trouble today.

But this was just a skirmish that he'd lost. The war could still be won. He was not about to turn his back on the case, not when that child, that precious child who'd been manipulated into playing accomplice after the fact, remained in the grip of a woman who, to March, for all her beauty, was a human cancer.

A cancer somebody had to cut out.

Jessica Ann, her hand lost in the big comforting grasp of Mr. Ekhardt, walked down the hallway to where Mommy was pacing, black heels clicking on the marble floor. The woman was clearly nervous as she smoked her cigarette, indifferent to the building's no-smoking rule.

The child was slightly amazed; she'd never seen her mother smoke, had no idea her mother had ever smoked, though from time to time she'd smelled what she didn't realize was cigarette smoke in the house, thinking it was only some unpleasant cooking odor.

Jessica Ann was relieved the interrogation was over. She hadn't lied, not exactly. Nobody had asked her if she knew Mark was an investigator. Still, she felt funny about it. Guilty—like she'd let Mark down.

But Mark was dead, and beyond helping, and Mommy was alive, and was her mommy. . . .

The woman in black was moving to meet them as they approached.

"Do they have enough to hold me?" Mommy asked the attorney, falling in step with the man and child.

"Not yet," Mr. Ekhardt said. Suddenly he seemed tired.

Mommy's brow wrinkled. "What do you mean, 'not yet'?"

"I don't think this is going to let up," the attorney said, shaking his head. In the deposition room, he'd seemed energetic, now he seemed haggard and spent. "From the looks of that lieutenant in there, I'd say this little shindig is just starting. . . ."

Mommy moved closer to Mr. Ekhardt; she stroked his arm, smiled at him knowingly.

"Thank you, Neal," she said. "With you in our corner, I know we'll be just fine."

The attorney shook his head; he had a funny half-smile, and there was something strangely intimate in his tone as he said, "I'll say this much for you—you never give up. . . . Gotta give you that much. . . ."

The attorney glanced down at Jessica Ann, a glance that for just an instant seemed troubled; then he nodded at Mommy and strode off, his footsteps echoing down the courthouse hallway. As she watched him go, Mommy's warmly smiling expression dissolved into a cold, thoughtful frown.

When Jessica Ann got home, she changed into comfier clothes—blue jeans and a country-embroidered faux-jeweled denim top—and pony-tailed her hair back. This morning, Mommy had cleaned Jessica Ann's room—the police had taken the sheets and comforter and stuff away as evidence, and there was nothing but a white sheet covering the mattress, like the white sheet that had covered Mark on the stretcher—but the child didn't feel like spending much time there. She couldn't imagine sleeping on that bed; she couldn't even look at it without seeing Mark on his back, staring at the ceiling with his big surprised dead eyes.

Shuddering, she went to her mother's bedroom, to see how Mommy was doing—Mommy had been very quiet in the car coming home from the courthouse, her eyes flickering with thought—and the girl found her mother busy, packing.

Mommy had changed her clothes, too—this pantsuit with its beige pants and a beige and white checkered tunic top was about as casual as Mommy got. Clearly these were traveling clothes; clearly they were going to pick up and leave.

"Are we going somewhere, Mommy?" the child asked, sitting on the edge of her mommy's bed, on which a suitcase yawned open, receiving clothing Mommy was carrying to it from the closet.

"We're going on vacation, dear," Mommy said, patting the clothes in place.

"Where, Mommy?"

"To a foreign land," Mommy said sweetly, moving to the top drawer of the dresser. "It'll be a surprise."

"But . . . I have school—"

Mommy folded and patted clothing into the suitcase. "School gets out in a week or so. With your grades it won't matter. And then we'll put you in a wonderful new school."

The child's mind was reeling. "But what about my friends?"

Mommy's smile was both sweet and dismissive as she paused in her packing to touch Jessica Ann beneath the chin with her fingertips, lifting her face like a knickknack she was examining on a shelf.

"You'll make wonderful new friends, dear," Mommy said, and turned back to the dresser.

Jessica Ann's eyes widened as a chill of fear coursed through her: *Mommy was opening the sec-*

ond drawer, the drawer where the child had discovered the stolen plaque!

But as Mommy lifted from the drawer her lace and satin underthings, with their straps and flaps and disturbingly sexual connotations, carrying them to the suitcase as casually as if they were a pile of newspapers, the child realized, to her sudden relief, that the plaque was no longer there.

The child sighed, settling herself back down. Mommy was a lot of things, but she wasn't a fool. The award was probably in the river by now.

From under the bed, Mommy withdrew a smaller suitcase and deposited it before her daughter.

"Here, dear," she said. "Take this and go pack your own things."

"But . . . what about my stuffed animals?"

Patiently, Mommy said, "Pick your favorite. Aunt Beth will send the others along when we get where we're going."

"Okay, Mommy."

Wearily, the child moved from the bed, reached down for the suitcase, and looked up to see her smiling mother, hands behind her back, in the all-too-familiar posture.

"Who's your best friend?" Mommy said brightly.

Jessica Ann heaved a sigh. "You are."

"Who loves you—"

"You do," Jessica Ann cut in sullenly, and trudged out, almost dragging the suitcase. She didn't see her mother's tiny reaction to this near insolence, a frown followed by a shrug as the woman got quickly back to work.

In her own room, Jessica Ann dejectedly moved her clothing from her dresser to the suitcase, which lay on the bed about where Mark had fallen, and neatly packed her things. She knew it wasn't a vacation. She knew they were moving. What could she do about it?

Every kid knows that when your parents decide to move, the kid has no say in it, she thought. *You just go where they go. . . .*

She paused in her packing to survey her little menagerie of stuffed animals, sitting propped against a white pillow where Mommy had carefully arranged them; they looked at the child with wide sewn-on eyes, faces full of hope, as if each was making a case for its selection. The sad-faced, pointy-headed blue clown seemed to be trying to force a smile to win her favor. But there was no contest: Teddy was the victor, hands down. She plucked him from the little group and placed him on his back near the suitcase, where his wide button eyes stared at the ceiling. She patted his head soothingly, as her eyes caught sight of something gleaming on the wall over her desk, the late-afternoon sunlight reflecting off of them: the award plaques.

Without pause, certainly without the careful consideration she'd given her stuffed animals, the girl lifted the first plaque off its nail and tossed it into the wastebasket below with a *clunk*. The second plaque went just as quickly, though she studied the third for just a moment, the words OUTSTANDING STUDENT freezing her momentarily. The child thought that maybe she should save one of the awards, then immediately realized that these were nothing she ever wanted to see again, and tossed the final one to its wastebasket resting place, where it *clunked* on top of the others, amid the yellow and black crime-scene tape that Mommy had removed from blocking her doorway.

Finally she moved to her nightstand and picked up the I ♥ DADDY framed photo, held it lovingly in her hands. Then she walked it over to the open suitcase and looked at Daddy's smiling bearded face and said, "This time you have to go where *I* tell you, Daddy."

And she packed him carefully away in the suitcase, between some nice soft clothes, so Daddy wouldn't get broken. The child thought of one other memento she would like to take, but it was downstairs, and she wondered if she should take time to go down and get it. . . .

They drove for a long time, for several hours, leaving the house on Rockwell Road behind, leaving McKinley School behind, and Ferndale itself, driving until dusk gave way to dark, and then driving some more. There was little talk, and Jessica Ann rested but didn't think she'd ever quite fallen asleep. Mommy listened to the radio, that '70s music she liked, only when a love song came on, she snapped the radio off like it had done something bad to her.

It must have been close to midnight when

Mommy pulled the sleek blue Cadillac in and up to the convenience store's self-service gas pumps; she talked some man in a plaid shirt and a Kent Feeds cap into filling the car for her, while she went inside to get some coffee for herself and some cocoa for Jessica Ann. The two females sat in the car and sipped their warm cups while the man filled the car. Mother and daughter smiled at each other, occasionally, like strangers being polite.

Finally, Mommy got out and thanked the man, who was looking at her like she was a meal and he was hungry, and went inside to pay for the gas. When Mommy came back out, purse tucked under her arm, she was smoking again, and as she moved toward the car, she seemed distracted, sort of slowing down; she dropped the cigarette to the pavement and ground it under her shoe. Watching her out the rider's side window, Jessica Ann felt her mommy looked . . . different. Not just the smoking, but something else. What was it?

Was Mommy frightened, too?

But as Mommy noticed Jessica Ann watching her, the funny look, a sort of blank apprehensive expression, disappeared, and a radiant smile took its place, a smile so beautiful, so reassuring, Jessica Ann could only smile back, love welling up inside of her for her mommy, despite it all.

Mommy got behind the wheel, started the car. "You about ready to stop, honey?"

"Could we, Mommy?" the child said hopefully. "Sleeping in the car makes my tummy hurt."

Mommy smiled and nodded. "We'll pull in at the next vacancy we see. . . ."

And as the mother pulled out, the child yawned, looking forward to a good night's sleep.

But when the next exit took them through an industrial area on the outskirts of some town, where the smokestacks of factories were filling the night with gray clouds, where the factories themselves loomed like jungles of twisted pipes and tubes and towers and shapes, past a sprawling junkyard that might have been fun to play in (in the daytime), Jessica Ann began to feel uneasy. That uneasiness grew to trepidation as her mother pulled down into the driveway of the Lamplighter, a motel whose main office had 1950s-style modern architecture of stark angles, highlighted by tiny colored spotlights in the grass that caused the structure to be draped in weird, sharp shadows and odd pools of color. The wings of the motel were one-story rows of doorways that were lost in darkness and in the shadowy shade of ghostly trees whose branches reached out as if to grab the child. The gravel parking lot had only a few cars, none of them nice like Mommy's Cadillac, but pickup trucks and dusty dirty cars of indiscriminate make.

This wasn't at all like the Marriotts and Radissons they usually stayed at on vacation; once in a while, Mommy would settle for a Holiday Inn or a Ramada Inn, but a rundown roach motel like this, on the edge of a town where the air smelled like dirty smoke . . . it just wasn't *like* Mommy. . . .

Jessica Ann hugged her teddy bear and closed her eyes. All she wanted was a nice soft warm bed. She didn't care if it was in this scary place. She didn't care at all.

That was what she kept telling herself, as her mommy went in to register.

Chapter Sixteen

Her mother opened the door, reaching in for the light switch, clicking on a lamp on a bureau at left. Then, suitcase in hand, Mommy stepped into the motel room, holding open the door for Jessica Ann, who trailed unsurely in, lugging both the teddy bear and her small suitcase.

"Well," Mommy said, sounding a little relieved, "this isn't so bad, is it?"

Jessica Ann, stopping at the foot of the first of two double beds with matching pinkish threadbare spreads, took in the shabby, sparsely furnished room, and shook her head, thinking, *This is awful*, saying, "No, Mommy."

The room did bask in an oddly golden glow from that bureau lamp, softening the harshness of its three cement-block walls. The other wall, against which the headboards of the beds rested, was cheap wood paneling. Outside, the rumble and wheezing and brake-squealing of passing trucks provided a constant backdrop. Over the bed Jessica Ann stood near was a portrait of a bullfighter in his cape with his sword, a cheap faded print in a heavy ornate frame; over the other bed, which Mommy was setting her suitcase on, was an equally faded portrait in a matching frame of a beautiful Spanish lady, in a low-cut dress, posing with a rose. Between the pictures, over the nightstand where Mommy had switched on another lamp, was a black plaque consisting of a sort of family crest with crossed swords.

"All right," Mommy said, "get your jammies on. . . ."

Jessica Ann nodded and hoisted her suitcase up onto the foot of the bed, as Mommy walked around behind her, setting the room key on the bureau. Then Mommy headed over to the other bed, sat on the edge of it, facing her daughter as the girl rustled in her suitcase. The mother, quietly preoccupied, unzipped her purse and withdrew her wallet and a thick envelope that looked like a fat letter.

First order of business for Jessica Ann was to take Daddy's picture out from its safe haven in the midst of her clothing, so that Daddy would be by her bedside, tonight as every night. As she carted the I ♥ DADDY frame to the nightstand, the child noticed her mother apparently checking over some official papers or something. She wondered what that was about.

The girl would have been surprised and, had she given it any thought at all, dismayed to know that her mother was examining a single, one-way airline ticket.

And, as the girl passed her mother, on the way back to her suitcase and jammies, Jessica Ann noticed her mommy looking in the wallet, checking over her driver's license. That struck the child as odd, but it would have struck her odder still if she'd seen that the driver's license, with her mother's picture on it, was made out to a false name, a name that was also on the social security card and several credit cards in that same wallet.

As Jessica Ann gathered her pajamas, slippers, and toiletries from the suitcase, her mommy was putting the wallet away in her purse, zippering it back shut. And when the child headed toward the bathroom, Mommy was sitting studying her wedding ring, kind of fiddling with it, like maybe it wasn't fitting her right any more. Or maybe she was thinking about Mr. Sterling, who gave it to her. Or maybe just contemplating the life they were leaving behind.

In her pajamas, with their blue bottoms and white top decorated with paisley hearts, Jessica Ann stood at the sink and brushed her teeth with thorough care; Mommy was a real stickler about dental hygiene. The child had eyeteeth that were coming in kind of funny, and she wondered what would happen to the braces she'd been fitted for, now that they were moving. She hoped she wouldn't have to start the painful process all over again.

Her mother called out to her, "How's my angel doing?"

Emerging from the bathroom, Jessica Ann found her mother turning down her daughter's bed, having set Teddy aside (the girl had tucked the toy in, like a little person).

"That's what Mark used to call me," Jessica Ann said, somewhat accusingly.

Mommy looked up as she smoothed back the sheet, then she looked away, fluffed the girl's pillow and said, "I miss him, too."

Then the mother guided her daughter into bed.

"Do you, Mommy?" the child asked, crawling under the covers.

Mommy was lifting the covers up around the girl, tucking her in. "I'm sorry . . . the accident . . . happened."

Did Mommy really believe that? Could she make herself believe that lie? Or did she just want to know if Jessica Ann believed it?

Mommy sat on the edge of the bed, just across from the child.

"Do you miss Daddy?"

A strange, crooked little smile formed on Mommy's pretty face; for a moment, she was someplace else, in some other time. "I miss Daddy most of all."

Jessica Ann yawned.

Her mommy leaned forward, the smile losing its

crookedness. "You probably aren't going to have any trouble getting to sleep tonight, are you?"

The child returned the smile, shook her head. "No, Mommy, I'm *really* tired."

Mommy looked at Jessica Ann for a long time, and the smile turned into a sort of frown, for just a second, and Mommy shook her head slowly, in that way a person does who's contemplating a sad situation about which nothing can be done.

Then Mommy rose and knelt by the child's bed, taking her daughter's hands in her own, and gazing at Jessica Ann with the most beautiful smile the child had ever been given by her mother, a smile that seemed to have a lot of things in it—happiness, sorrow, pride, regret. Jessica Ann couldn't quite sort it all out, but it was a special smile, a smile to look back on and cherish.

"Do you know how proud I am of you?" Mommy asked softly, tenderly. "For being such a good student? And such a good girl?"

Jessica Ann returned her mother's smile, but something about the smile confused her, and she glanced at the picture of Daddy, as if for support or advice.

Then Mommy was leaning in to kiss her daughter on the forehead.

The gesture warmed Jessica Ann's heart; this, and the words her mother had just spoken, were like some wonderful gift the woman was bestowing upon her. What had Jessica Ann done to deserve this?

Daughter smiled up at mother, mother smiled down at daughter.

"Say your prayers, dear," Mommy said.

The child nodded, said her prayers, said goodnight to Daddy, and settled down to sleep; but Mommy didn't get dressed for bed, or get under the covers. Though she did reach out and turn off the nightstand lamp, Mommy had settled herself on the edge of the bed, right across from Jessica Ann, sitting there fiddling with the wedding ring, and wringing her hands, as the child drifted off.

Jessica Ann slept soundly, deeply, and she dreamed. She dreamed she was in her room in the house on Rockwell Road, but everything had an eerie green glow and fog floated like factory smoke, distorting and concealing. She was standing facing her bed, and Mark was there, dead, sprawled on his back, staring at the ceiling with his wide dead eyes, those awful splotches of red on his shirt.

She didn't like looking at him, dead like that, but she couldn't move. She was rooted in one spot. Glued to the floor.

And then slowly, Mark began to sit up; like a robot somebody switched on, he sat erect, his eyes still wide and dead, then he seemed to relax, as if air had suddenly been breathed back into him. He looked at her, right at her, and his eyes were alive again, his face was alive, and he spoke to her.

"She's a sick person," he said. "And she needs to be stopped. And she needs to be helped."

The message in the dream startled her awake. On

her side, with her back to her mommy's bed, she lay frozen, eyes wide, disturbed by the dream, which still vividly filled her mind. She was not aware that behind her, on the edge of the other bed, sat her mother, who had been sitting there, watching the child, studying her, coming to some terrible private decision through the long night.

Upsetting as the dream was, it began to fade, and her tiredness won out over its message, and she settled herself back down to go back to sleep. Her mother, unaware that the child was awake, began to speak very softly.

"Sometimes mommies have to make hard decisions. . . ."

The child's eyes opened wide again.

". . . If they took Mommy away . . ." She made a disgusted dismissive sniff. ". . . who would look after you?"

Jessica Ann knew Mommy was telling her these things only because Mommy didn't know she was awake and could hear them. . . .

The girl didn't budge in the bed, even though she sensed her mommy rising behind her, even though the shadow of the woman's raised hands, cupped together, fell upon her and her pillow, hands held out as if in an offering of compassionate help, only now the fingers began to splay, to claw, as if preparing to grasp and choke. . . .

When she sensed her mommy just above her, the child squealed and sprang from the bed, bolting toward the door, as her mother, grunting with irritation and frustration, flopped bodily onto the bed where the daughter had been.

Jessica Ann fumbled with the night latch, got it undone, and was pulling open the door when Mommy was there, right on top of her, slamming the door, her hand raising in a sweeping blow that sent the child ducking when all Mommy was doing was hitting the light switch, flooding the room with blinding illumination.

The child slipped out from under her, yelping, "Mommy!" looking back wild-eyed as she scrambled toward the the closed bathroom door, yanking it open, stealing herself inside, slamming the door, locking the door, her mother a half-second behind.

"Jessica Ann." Her mother was rattling the knob. "Jessica *Ann*!"

The child faced the blank whiteness of the door, pleading with it, touching the trim of a door panel as if kneeling at the hem of a holy garment. "Don't, Mommy! Don't! Leave me alone. . . ."

"Jessica Ann," Mommy said, voice raised but not angry, "open the door . . ."

"No!"

"You just had a bad dream, dear—a nightmare." Mommy's voice was firm but reasonable. "Now . . . open the door."

"No way!" The sobbing child looked every which way around the little bathroom, desperately getting her bearings.

"Come out and we'll go back to sleep, now. . . ."

She had to get out of this little room. Her eyes

fixed upon the window next to the stool, its blue curtains beckoning.

"We have a big day tomorrow, Jessica Ann," Mommy's voice said musically through the door. "A lot of driving . . . I need my good little navigator. . . ."

Her little blue rubber-soled slippers were on a stand near the window; she'd brought them in when she brushed her teeth, but hadn't worn them in to bed!

The knob was rattling again, and her mother's voice contorted as she said, *"Open the door!"*

Jessica Ann sat on the lid of the stool and pulled on the slippers, quick as a bunny. Her mother had stopped rattling the doorknob, and had stopped trying to reason with her, too; it was disturbingly quiet out there. The child stood on the toilet-seat lid and brushed aside the curtains to get at the window. She unlocked it and tried to slide the heavy pane to one side; it was stuck. Putting all her little weight into it, she finally budged the thing, and slid it whiningly open.

She was just going out the window when her mother's fist came crashing through the door panel, the power of her blow popping most of the panel out in one piece, splintering the rest, and Mommy leaned through the opening and reached in to unlock the door, opening it just as her daughter was slipping down to the ground and fleeing into the night.

Chapter Seventeen

The child ran.

Climbing from the window took her to the rear of the motel, between the wings of the low-slung structure, and she went scurrying through a courtyard area of picnic tables and drooping shade trees, their branches bending down, throwing puddles of shadow, shadows that seemed to move. Jessica Ann slowed to a trot, tucked herself behind a tree to catch her breath, trying to get her bearings.

From here she could get a side view of the motel; the front office was dark, just as every window in every room of the Lamplighter was dark, and the highway—which earlier had teemed with trucks—seemed deserted now. Across the way a factory loomed, hurling smoke into the sky; had she not been eleven years old, it might have occurred to her that there were people working in that factory she might turn to. But as she panted against the tree, her eyes darting like a frightened animal's, she saw only spires of smoke and dark uninviting shapes.

"Jessica Ann!"

Still tucked behind the tree, the child glanced back and across the picnic area, where she could see the bathroom window and Mommy framed there, leaning out, her face distorted with fury.

And Jessica Ann knew in that terrible moment that the only people in this nighttime world were her mother and herself. She could only do what any child would do: run and hide.

"Jessica Ann, come back here this instant!"

As the girl ran, skirting the motel's TV satellite dish, she caught sight of the wooded area beyond, a natural hiding place. It was as forbidding as the factory, though a glow of light from behind the trees held out hope for a brighter world than the one she was fleeing through. Her tiny slippered feet sprinted across the mowed lawn of the courtyard and into high uncut grass, which slowed her to a trot. She craned her neck back and, far away but not far enough away, saw her mommy climbing down out of that bathroom window.

The tall grass mingled with stiff stalky weeds further slowed the girl's movement. Her breaths indistinguishable from her sobs, the child slogged through the ever-higher, ever-stiffer blades, pushing on desperately as if she were swimming in underbrush. Glances behind her told her Mommy was coming.

Mommy wasn't running, she was striding, across the courtyard, into the higher grass, slapping the tall weeds aside impatiently, as if they too were disobedient children, her face now devoid of anything but cold rage, a pale white Kabuki mask in the moonlight.

Just as the weeds reached over the child's head—if they had been water she'd be drowning—they gave way to bushes that Jessica Ann gratefully disappeared into, even as the sounds behind her, crunching grass, crackling brush, announced her mother catching up. The girl's speed and smaller size were assets, but the woman pursuing her had shifted into stalking mode, her senses as alert and cunning as a beast of prey, eyes keen, ears sharp, nostrils flared, sniffing the air for the scent of her child.

Clawing through the bushes, getting nicked and pricked by brambles and thorns, her tears streaming, her hysteria mounting, the child found herself amid the trees she'd been running toward, the light beyond them filtering through. Hope springing, she weaved through their trunks until her hope caught in her throat as she stopped short, almost crashing into a high, rusty, chain-link fence. From behind her came the harsh whisper of her mother moving through the brush; and the child moved along the fence, little fingers clutching its links as she went, whimpering. The fence was shaking and shivering, as was she, as she followed it along, hand over little hand, gliding along it with peculiar grace, as if she were climbing it sideways, seeking the source of the light.

And then there her salvation was, rising beyond the chain-link barrier: the junkyard.

That scary Disneyland of a junkyard she and Mommy had passed on their way to the motel, caught in the moonlight, illuminated by yellow security lights on high posts, its mounds of rubble, its piles of refuse, its rows of dead cars, making a sort of a skyline in the night, a bizarre parody of a city.

Behind her, the sound of her mother cleaving through the bushes spurred Jessica Ann on, and the child jogged along the fence, little fingers clutching it, shaking it, testing it; then suddenly she found herself at a loose place in the rusty wire, and with a tug on either side, it made a perfect portal for her to slip through.

She did, too eagerly, and fell on the hard scrubby ground with an "Oooff!" inadvertently alerting her mother, who had begun moving along that chain-link fence herself, now, in steady pursuit.

The child got to her feet in a cloud of dirt and dust her fall had raised, and scurried down a pathway, rounding an immense mountain of rubble, of rotten boards, metal scraps, rusted-out metal drums, ancient washing machines, defunct refrigerators. As Jessica Ann looked about her, her wide eyes taking in this eerie graveyard of consumerism, her slippered feet did not slow down, despite the uncertain course she was charting. This hellish landscape seemed a questionable trade for the dark claustrophobia of the underbrush and trees she'd fled. Ground fog drifted; the full moon cast constant if shifting illumination, as dark clouds streaked over its silver-white face like black smoke.

Gasping for breath, the child paused at a pile of scrap metal, putting her hands on her knees, and as she swallowed, panting, preparing herself to get back on the move, she heard something *snap* very near her. She whirled—and a raccoon, rummaging through the rubble, moved by at a slow pace she could only envy.

Then she heard the rattle and creak that meant Mommy was coming through the fence.

The junkyard, like a town, was arranged in streets, at least this part of it was, and Jessica Ann turned down a lane on which either side of her towered racks of crushed cars, skeletal towers so tall their shadows blotted out the moonlight, the racked squashed cars looking down at her, their smashed, stacked faces staring at her, glaring at her with cracked and shattered eyes, as she raced down the pathway. Then she turned down another lane of dead cars, a lane where the skeleton racks cradled skeleton cars, the bare rusty chassis crouching like creatures about to leap; a shuddering chill coursed through her, and she cut down another lane, this one's racks piled on either side with crushed cars again, and soon she began losing any sense of where she was and where she'd been. She felt lost in a nightmare where each pathway leads to an endless other, a maze of grotesque trails leading nowhere you haven't already been, nowhere you wanted to be, leading back in on themselves unceasingly, and she thought of Snow White, lost in the forest. That was how she felt, everything around her growing faces, hovering over her with evil intent.

Finally a long wide path presented itself, with more dead cars lying like metal corpses in the weeds on either side, but at least she was out of those lanes of looming towers, at least the moonlight and security lights were paving a way, and she ran, ran for her life, and did not see her mother step into the mouth of the wide path and stand there for a moment, catching her own breath, her shadow chasing her daughter, fixing her eye on where the child was headed.

Jessica Ann rounded the corner, her tears finally abating, glad to be in a more open area; here cars in better shape sat side by side in rows, sitting in weedy spots like a used car lot positioned in an open field. But in front of her were more mountains of rubble, and it occurred to Jessica Ann that one of these cars might make a good place to hide. How, in this endless ocean of dead vehicles, could her mother hope to find the one car the child chose?

Coming to a stop, ready to make a decision, the girl glanced around her. Ahead were those mountains of rubble, to her left were more lanes of skeletal racks of crushed cars. To her right were two enormous piles of uncrushed cars, two three-story walls of uncrushed car bodies, one after another stacked atop each other, coming together in a wide V; nearby rose the crane that had no doubt accomplished this Stonehenge of steel.

And next to that cliff of piled cars, within the shelter of its V, was one car that had either fallen from above or that the crane hadn't gotten round to lifting yet, a car in fairly good condition, sitting in the shadow of the Stonehenge, its door yawning open as if inviting her in.

She took the invitation, scurrying to the junker, slipping behind the wheel, as if she were driving, and shutting the door, then peeking out the window to see if Mommy was coming. A metallic *clunk* at her right caught her attention, and she did not see her mommy come up and stand where Jessica Ann had stood moments before, when the child had looked around to make her decision where to hide.

When Jessica Ann did turn her head, and did see her mommy, who was staring straight ahead at the mountain range of rubble, the child ducked down, her ponytail flopping, a fraction of a second before Mommy turned to look at what was just another dead car in a vast automotive cemetery.

Cowering in the front seat, the roughness of pebbled safety glass on the seat rubbing against and tearing her jammies, the child listened as her mommy's footsteps moved quickly away, and then faded entirely.

Jessica Ann waited what seemed like forever, but was only a few seconds, and then, placing one little hand at a time on the door where the window was rolled down, she pulled herself up and peeked out, just the top of her head showing.

No Mommy in sight.

Sighing, trying to decide what to do next, her tears ready to flow again at any moment, the child sat back behind the wheel, as if she were about to start the car and drive away, and didn't she wish she could. . . .

She wondered if she should just stay put until dawn, when maybe the men who worked here could help her, but right now she knew Mommy was gone, Mommy was off looking in the other direction. So if she went back the way Mommy came, maybe Jessica Ann could find her way out of the junkyard, and find some help *now*. . . .

So the child carefully, quietly, opened the car door, pushing it wide enough for her to crawl out, soundlessly dropping her slippered feet to the cindered ground, and looked ahead, where Mommy had disappeared, seeing nothing, and looked behind her, seeing nothing, and—being a good girl—she closed the car door. It made a sharp *click*, not very loudly, but enough to startle the girl, and she looked all around her again to see if the noise would stir Mommy's attention and send her back in this direction . . . but it didn't seem to have. Her eyes searching a horizon broken only by refuse mountains, she backed away from the car.

Then, relieved, she turned, bumping into her mother, standing right behind her.

"Just what do you think you're *doing*, young lady?"

And the child froze under the fury of her mother's countenance staring down at her, eyes like focused beams of wrath, the chiseled features of her beautiful heart-shaped face contorting into an elongated hideous mask whose every feature was blade-sharp: nose, cheekbones, chin, framed by sickles of swinging ice-blond hair.

But before the child could summon an answer to her mother's question, a sound from a nearby lane of dead cars drew both of their attention away, an ominous sound from the darkness of the nearby shadowed lane.

Growling.

Deep, belligerent, persistent growling, and from the darkness came eyes, green transparent eyes, demonic eyes that moved forward as if floating disembodied orbs, until the brown of his snout and legs began to reveal an animal shape emerging from the darkness, until the black of the muscular rest of the pit bull was apparent in the moonlight. His head was at least as big as Jessica Ann's, his torso thick and tubular, and his growls were turning into snarls; vicious fanglike teeth bared, saliva dripping, the heavy metal-studded collar around his neck with its steel tag made clanking sounds as he lumbered toward mother and daughter, standing together, united again, in mutual apprehension, petrified, as the snarls escalated to furious deep spit-flecked barks.

"Shit," Mommy said, and then she looked at Jessica Ann and shoved the girl aside, her expression telling the child to go, and as the lumbering dog picked up its speed to a trot, heading toward Mommy, she held up a hand, saying, "Stay!"

But it did no good.

As Jessica Ann moved away, Mommy tried to run behind the car that her daughter had hidden in, but the dog followed, the dog was on her, lunging at her, dragging the woman down and behind the car, as the night filled with the howls of both the animal and the woman, Mommy's cries of distress and pain overshadowed by the savage growls and ripping cloth.

In fear, and at her mother's bidding, the child ran, ran away, but the awful sounds stopped her and she looked back, and to her horror, through the windows of the dead car behind which that dog was attacking her mother, Jessica Ann could see glimpses of her mommy's pink flesh streaked with red, her hand, her arm, her face, bloody limbs flailing as the black-brown shape dragged her down.

When the child ducked behind the Stonehenge of cars, she peeked out and could see Mommy's scarlet hand slide slowly down the window, leaving a sort of awful red paw print, and as Mommy's moaning faded, the growling of the dog subsided too, and there was only silence.

"Mommy?" the child asked tentatively, crouching behind the edge of the far wall of stacked cars, then sobbing, she ventured, "Mommy!"

Silence.

Was that dog still there? Was Mommy alive? If she was, Mommy would need help, medical help . . . but hadn't Mommy been trying to hurt Jessica Ann? In the quietness, broken only by the chirping of cicadas, the child began to question what had happened. Had it all been only a bad dream, like Mommy said? Had the nightmare about Mark made her only *think* Mommy wanted to hurt her?

Hadn't Mommy pushed her aside, tried to save her, when that horrible dog charged at them, and hadn't Mommy given herself, maybe even her life, to take on that dog's attack, rather than have Jessica Ann endangered?

A calm settled over the child. She had to see if Mommy was still alive. She had to help Mommy, if she could. But that dog might still be around; he might be hovering over Mommy's . . . she hated even to frame the thought . . . over Mommy's body, right now. Jessica Ann had a terrible fleeting horror-movie image of the beast feeding on her mother's flesh, and she knew she had to try to help.

Looking around on the rubble-strewn ground where she crouched, the child found a pipe . . . but it was rubber, and not substantial enough, some kind of auto hose. A rock, a chunk of glass, a broken windshield wiper . . . no.

Then she spotted it, near the tire of the car she was kneeling by: a rusty iron pipe, not very big, but big enough. It fit her hand nicely. She could swing with this and *hurt* that dog, if she had to.

Cautiously, carefully, she rose from her crouch and moved gingerly around the edge of the wall of autos, and toward the car behind which Mommy and the dog had done battle. She held the pipe before her like a flare; she had never held any object with intent to use it as a weapon in her life. Uncertainly, she crept behind the car.

And found the body.

Obviously dead.

Neck broken.

The pit bull.

"*Now* do you see why I'd never let you have a dog?" Mommy asked, stepping from the darkness, gesturing to the dead animal.

Whirling, Jessica Ann tucked the pipe behind her as she faced her approaching mommy, whose beige pantsuit was shredded, hanging in tatters, soaked with blood. Mommy's face was streaked with blood as well, and the flesh of her forearms was ribboned with crimson, but there was something triumphant in her bearing.

"Mommy . . . don't," the child whimpered, backpedaling. "Please don't . . ."

Her wonderful smile clearly crazed now, Mommy moved forward, and Jessica Ann kept backing up until she had to stop, until she bumped the wall of cars behind her. Her mother had backed her into the corner, where the walls converged, trapping her there.

"This hurts me," Mommy said almost regretfully, moving closer, "more than it does you, dear. . . ."

"Yes, Mommy," the child said, and with all her might, she brought that pipe out from behind her in a roundhouse swing that whacked her mother alongside the head, sending the woman reeling, her perfect hair finally mussed.

For a moment, Jessica Ann thought her mother might topple.

Not Mommy.

Instead, the woman righted herself with a sort of shrug, looking at her daughter with surprise, perhaps a little pleased by the girl's gumption.

Then with a little regal shake of her head to clear the uncharacteristically messy hair from her line of vision, Mommy smiled the dazzling smile, even as a new trail of blood trickled from the corner of her mouth, from Jessica Ann's blow.

Again the mother began moving inexorably forward, and the daughter, cornered, dropped the pipe to the ground. What good would such a meager defense do against a force of nature like this? You couldn't stop Dracula so easily, or the Frankenstein monster, or the Mummy.

Or Mommy.

Maybe if Mommy didn't want her to live, Jessica Ann didn't want to be alive.

And now, with Jessica Ann backed up against the wall of cars, where the darkness was almost complete but for a shaft of moonlight spotlighting through, Mommy, slightly unsteadily, was lifting her hand to her heart in the familiar gesture.

"Who loves you," Mommy asked sadly, sincerely,

"more than anything on God's green earth?"

Sobbing, face wet with tears, Jessica Ann lifted her hand to her heart and nodded, saying, "You do, Mommy."

Mommy nodded gravely, and there was nothing mean in her face, in fact this was as loving a look as Jessica Ann could remember ever seeing from her mommy, as the woman bent down close to her daughter, showing the child open, cupped, giving hands, hands that came up as if to caress the child.

But the hands did not caress, they gripped, they seized upon the child's slender white throat, clamping tightly, and powerful fingers began to squeeze, and as Jessica Ann choked, struggling to breathe without success, tears glistening on her cheeks, she looked up at her mother and saw that all the beauty had drained from the woman's face and there, in its place, was the face of an animal, the scowling, growling, misshapen visage of a creature fueled only by a relentless will to do whatever was necessary to survive.

The child tried to pull her mother's hands off by grabbing onto her forearms, but it did no good. She closed her eyes, letting darkness in—she couldn't bear to see her mother's face like that, and the moonlight that washed her own face was too glaring to endure. But had she kept her eyes open, the child would have seen something remarkable pass across her mother's face.

The grimace that gripped her mother's features as tightly as her mother's hands gripped the girl's neck suddenly began to relax, to thaw into uncertainty, to betray a twinge of heartache. . . .

And to the child's amazement, the hands slowly, almost tenderly, withdrew . . . and Jessica Ann gasped for breath, tiny hands flying to her neck, rubbing where it hurt, tears exploding into full-blown sobbing, surprised, relieved, looking up into a face that was beautiful again.

The gunshot made them both jump.

As the shot echoed in the night, Mommy whirled, Jessica Ann looking past her, and there was Lieutenant March, his gun in the air, standing at the mouth of that lane from which the junkyard dog had emerged. He looked angry, coldly angry; it was an expression that Jessica Ann wouldn't have been surprised to see her mommy wear.

"Jessica Ann, move away from your mother!" the policeman called out.

And the child scampered away, huddling back around the corner of the wall of cars, where she'd hidden during the attack by the dog.

But Lieutenant March wasn't moving toward Mommy to arrest her, he was just standing there, pointing the gun at her, and they were exchanging looks across the distance that frightened the child, Mommy sneering at him, the detective frowning at her.

Then Lieutenant March raised the gun and mumbled something, something that Jessica Ann didn't think she was meant to hear: "I'm gonna do the world a favor. . . ."

She knew what that meant.

The child rushed to him, right up next to him, and she reached up and put her hand on his arm, right by his wrist, and, as best she could, she applied pressure. The policeman looked down at her and she looked up at him and shook her head, no, no, no, and the policeman's eyes got funny and then he swallowed and sort of sighed.

Then the arm Jessica Ann was pushing on drifted down, like a scale balancing, and the policeman looked at her a long time, stroking her hair.

Mommy just stood back in the corner of the car walls, waiting, but her chin was high. She didn't have her hands up or anything. She still had her pride.

"It's okay!" Lieutenant March called out to somebody, slipping his gun in its holster under his arm. "Come on."

Then Aunt Beth was there, bending to gather Jessica Ann into her arms, holding the child at arm's length, saying, "Are you all right, Jess?"

"I . . . I think so," Jessica Ann managed.

"You are one brave girl," she said admiringly. Aunt Beth was smiling, but Jessica Ann didn't believe the smile—her aunt's eyes were too sad, and her mouth was quivering, like she was holding back tears.

Jessica Ann didn't bother holding hers back.

"What . . . what are you *doing* here, Aunt Beth?"

"Lieutenant March was keeping your mother under surveillance," Aunt Beth said, slipping her arm around the child's shoulders, beginning to walk her away to the front area of the junkyard, where a police car could drive them back to the motel. "We were out front, in that factory's parking lot, and I'd fallen asleep—"

"Aunt Beth . . ."

"What, Jess?"

"Can I live with you, now? I don't want to go to a new school."

Aunt Beth's laugh was surprised and sort of sad. "Of course you can."

"Good," the child said, unaware that shock was beginning to settle in. "I like my school."

Aunt Beth, swallowing back tears, stroked Jessica Ann's hair soothingly as they walked along. "It's over now, Jessy. It's over."

"She couldn't do it, Aunt Beth," Jessica Ann said, crying, but feeling strangely happy, somehow.

"I know, honey," Aunt Beth said, drawing the girl even closer.

"Mommy *does* love me!"

On this terrible night, with her neck red and raw and aching from her mother's touch, Jessica Ann had learned something that now and forever would warm the cold memories. The child lifted her chin, walking along proudly. Her mommy had done a lot of bad things, but she couldn't bring herself to kill *her* little girl.

The child didn't hear the exchange between her mother and the detective, back at the Stonehenge of cars, where March was handcuffing his prisoner's hands behind her.

"Why didn't you do it?" he asked her. "She was the only one who could really testify against you. . . . Why'd you hesitate?"

She didn't seem to know herself, at first, and she looked up at the sky, for the answer.

"For a moment there . . . in the moonlight," Mrs. Sterling said, her confusion transforming itself into a regal if bloodied and typically dazzling smile, "she looked like *me*. . . ."

And the cop yanked the handcuffed woman rudely around, to walk her to the waiting car in the light of a full moon whose pure whiteness was visible only intermittently through the brocade of black clouds drifting across its blank face.

Chapter Eighteen

At the Lamplighter, in the motel room, Beth helped her niece gather her things. She didn't even bother to have the girl get out of the pajamas; they would be going directly to the emergency room of the hospital in the nearby town so the child could be examined, and her cuts and bruises tended to. She wondered if her sister would be going there, as well, or if they had their own medical facilities at the jail.

Jessica Ann was taking the I ♥ DADDY picture from the nightstand as Beth stood at the foot of the bed, near the child's suitcase, thinking that she could never forgive her sister, and that she could never forgive herself for allowing this child to remain in harm's way. Beth was trembling with anger when the girl returned to her suitcase to tuck her father's framed picture away. When the child lifted her folded clothing to pack the picture, another picture was revealed.

Jessica Ann glanced up at her aunt and removed the second framed photo, a studio portrait of her mother, smiling, beautiful, perfect in her pearls. The child gazed beseechingly at her aunt, as if asking permission to still love her mother, and a bittersweet rush went through Beth and she swallowed and nodded and hugged the girl to her.

The child placed the photo of her mommy in the suitcase, next to the one of her daddy, the other parent she'd lost, and carefully, lovingly, protectively surrounded them with her folded garments. Then the girl went into the bathroom, past the splintered door, to gather her toiletries.

A knock summoned them outside, where Lieutenant March had already placed the child's mother in back of one of two state police patrol cars that waited, their flashing lights casting a red glow on the proceedings. March, who had his own unmarked car here of course, was staying close to the vehicle that bore his prisoner.

Beth was startled by the contrast between the perfect mother in Jessica Ann's framed photo and the tousle-haired, haggard, blood-streaked face of the woman in the back of the patrol car.

Just as a state police officer was opening the back door of the other patrol car for Beth and Jessica Ann, taking their bags from them politely, the car bearing the girl's mommy began to pull away.

And framed in the window of the patrol car,

Beth's sister turned to look at her, and look at the child in dirty torn pajamas standing there next to Beth, clutching her teddy bear, and, though Beth couldn't be sure, she thought she saw something strangely human in the face, something atypically reflective, even regretful.

Then Beth glanced toward Jessica Ann and saw what may have prompted this humanity on the part of her sister.

Jessica Ann, her lovely tear-streaked face full of unconditional love, was standing with her hand over her heart, sending her mother one last message as she was taken away.

Editor Don D'Auria suggested that those who enjoy the novel Mommy *(and my film version of it) might find the original short story of interest, and we include it here as a sort of appendix to this, the first edition of the novel.*

In 1994 I was invited to contribute a short story to an anthology entitled Fear Itself. *Jeff Gelb, the anthology's editor—and cocreator of the best-selling* Hot Blood *and* Shock Rock *series—invited a number of authors who specialized in suspense and horror to reveal, by way of a short story, their own "ultimate fear." To some degree I fudged, because to tell you the truth, fear of heights—that is, vertigo—is probably really my biggest fear; but Alfred Hitchcock seemed to have already taken that one (and probably, by way of his film of that title, planted the seeds of that fear in me, when I saw it at about the age of Jessica Ann in this story).*

The notion of doing a mother-daughter "switch" on The Bad Seed *was something I'd been kicking around for some time, and a short (three-page) synopsis of* Mommy *as a screenplay was one of several projects being considered by a group of us for production as an independent film. When Jeff Gelb offered me the invitation into* Fear Itself, *I used that opportunity to flesh out the little synopsis into a short story. This story was what sparked Patty McCormack's interest in doing our film.*

The story is remarkably similar to the novel and the film, reflecting the fact that this was a tale that came to me whole, full-blown, like a vividly remembered dream (even that three-page synopsis contains such key pieces of dialogue as, "For a moment there in the moonlight . . . she looked like me"). You will notice that one murder is missing (the death of the janitor, which is an overt, albeit sex-changed, reference to the similar character, Leroy, in The Bad Seed*) and that the time of year is Christmas. Though it's not overly emphasized, the ironic Christmas setting is a loss I do regret in the longer, "final" versions of this story (prompted by the fact that we shot the film in summer). Other details differ—in the story, the school is named after a different assassinated president, for example—but the fable of Jessica Ann and her mommy remains, at its heart, inviolate. It has always been my intention that this tale be both dark* and *sweet, which is why some people like it so much—and others just don't get it.*

"Mommy" the short story was nicely received, winning inclusion in the Mystery Scene *magazine* The Year's 25 Finest Crime and Mystery Stories *anthology. Following the story is a brief essay on the subject of the fear explored in "Mommy," a coda that was a part of every tale in Gelb's fine* Fear Itself *anthology.*

The mother and daughter in the hallway of John F. Kennedy Grade School were each other's picture-perfect reflection.

Mommy wore a tailored pink suit with high heels, her blond hair short and perfectly coiffed; pearls caressed the shapely little woman's pale throat, and a big black purse was tucked under her arm. Daughter, in a frilly white blouse with a pink skirt and matching tights, was petite, too, a head smaller than her mother. Their faces were almost identical—heart-shaped, with luminous china-blue eyes, long lashes, cupid's-bow mouths, and creamy complexions.

The only difference between them was Mommy's serene, madonnalike countenance; the little girl was frowning. The frown was not one of disobedience—Jessica Ann Sterling was as well-behaved a modern child as you might hope to find—but a frown of frustration.

"Please don't, Mommy," she said. "I don't want you to make Mrs. Withers mad at me."

"It's only a matter of what's fair," Mommy said. "You have better grades than that little foreign student."

"He's not foreign, Mommy. Eduardo is Hispanic, and he's a good student, too."

"Not as good as you." Mommy's smile was a beautiful thing; it could warm up a room. "The award is for 'Outstanding Student of the Year.' You have straight A's, perfect attendance, you're the best student in the 'Talented and Gifted' group."

"Yes, Mommy, but—"

"No 'buts,' dear. *You* deserve the 'Outstanding Student' award. Not this little Mexican."

"But Mommy, it's just a stupid plaque. I don't need another. I got one last year . . ."

"And the year before, and the year before that—and you deserve it again this year. Perhaps it's best you go out and wait in the car for Mommy." She looked toward the closed door of the fifth-grade classroom. "Perhaps this should be a private conference."

"Mommy, please don't embarrass me."

"I would never do that. Now. Who's your best friend?"

"You are, Mommy."

"Who loves you more than anything on God's green earth?"

"You do, Mommy."

The little girl, head lowered, shuffled down the hall.

"Jessica Ann . . ."

She turned, hope springing. "Yes, Mommy?"

Mommy shook her finger in the air, gently. "Posture."

"Yes, Mommy."

And the little girl went out to wait in their car.

Mrs. Thelma Withers knew that trimming her room with Christmas decorations probably wasn't politically correct, but she was doing it, anyway. She had checked with Levi's parents, to see if they objected, and they said as long as there were no "Christian symbols" displayed, it was okay.

For that reason, she had avoided images of Santa Claus—technically, at least, he was "Saint Nicholas," after all—but what harm could a little silver tinsel around the blackboard do?

The portly, fiftyish teacher was on a stepladder

stapling the ropes of tinsel above the blackboard when Mrs. Sterling came in.

Looking over her shoulder, Mrs. Withers said, "Good afternoon, Mrs. Sterling. I hope you don't mind if I continue with my decorating . . ."

"We did have an appointment for a conference."

What a pain this woman was. The child, Jessica Ann, was a wonderful little girl, and a perfect student, but the mother—what a monster! In almost thirty years of teaching, Thelma had never had one like her—constantly pestering her about imagined slights to her precious child.

"Mrs. Sterling, we had our conference for the quarter just last week. I really want to have these decorations up for the children, and if you don't mind, we'll just talk while—"

"I don't mind," the woman said coldly. She was standing at the desk, staring at the shining gold wall plaque for "Outstanding Student of the Year" that was resting there. Her face was expressionless, yet there was something about the woman's eyes that told Thelma Withers just how covetous of the award she was.

Shaking her head, Mrs. Withers turned back to her work, stapling the tinsel in place.

The *click clack* of the woman's high heels punctuated the sound of stapling as Mrs. Sterling approached.

"You're presenting that plaque tonight, at the PTA meeting," she said.

"That's right," Mrs. Withers said, her back still to the woman.

"You *know* that my daughter deserves that award."

"Your daughter is a wonderful student, but so is Eduardo Melindez."

"Are his grades as good as Jessica Ann's?"

Mrs. Withers stopped stapling and glanced back at the woman, literally looking down her nose at Jessica Ann's mother.

"Actually, Mrs. Sterling, that's none of your business. How I arrive at who the 'Outstanding Student' is is my affair."

"Really."

"Really. Eduardo faces certain obstacles your daughter does not. When someone like Eduardo excels, it's important to give him recognition."

"Because he's a Mexican, you're taking the award away from my daughter? You're punishing her for being white, and for coming from a nice family?"

"That's not how I look at it. A person of color like Eduardo—"

"You're not going to give the award to Jessica, are you?"

"It's been decided."

"There's no name engraved on the plaque. It's not too late."

With a disgusted sigh, Mrs. Withers turned and glared at the woman. "It is too late. What are you teaching your daughter with this behavior, Mrs. Sterling?"

"What are you teaching her, when you take what's rightfully hers and give it to somebody because he's a 'person of color'?"

"I don't have anything else to say to you, Mrs. Sterling. Good afternoon." And Mrs. Withers turned back to her stapling, wishing she were stapling this awful woman's head to the wall.

It was at that moment that the ladder moved, suddenly, and the teacher felt herself losing balance, and falling, and she tumbled through the air and landed on her side, hard, the wind knocked out of her.

Moaning, Mrs. Withers opened her eyes, trying to push herself up. Her eyes were filled with the sight of Mrs. Sterling leaning over her, to help her up.

She thought.

Jessica Ann watched as one of the JFK front doors opened and Mommy walked from the building to the BMW, her big purse snugged tightly to her. Mommy wore a very serious expression, almost a frown.

Mommy opened the car door and leaned in.

"Is something wrong?" Jessica Ann asked.

"Yes," she said. "There's been a terrible accident . . . when I went to speak to Mrs. Withers, she was lying on the floor."

"On the floor?"

"She'd been up a ladder, decorating the room for you children. She must have been a very thoughtful teacher."

"Mommy, you make it sound like . . ."

"She's dead, dear. I think she may have broken her neck."

"Mommy . . ." Tears began to well up. Jessica Ann thought the world of Mrs. Withers.

"I stopped at the office and had the secretary phone for an ambulance. I think we should stay around until help comes, don't you?"

"Yes, Mommy."

An ambulance came very soon, its siren screaming, but for no reason: When Mrs. Withers was wheeled out on a stretcher, she was all covered up. Jessica bit her finger and watched and tried not to cry. Mommy stood beside her, patting her shoulder.

"People die, dear," Mommy said. "It's a natural thing."

"What's natural about falling off a ladder, Mommy?"

"Is that a smarty tone?"

"No, Mommy."

"I don't think Mrs. Withers would want you speaking to your mother in a smarty tone."

"No, Mommy."

"Anyway, people fall off ladders all the time. You know, more accidents occur at home than anywhere else."

"Mrs. Withers wasn't at home."

"The workplace is the next most frequent."

"Can we go now?"

"No. I'll need to speak to these gentlemen."

A police car was pulling up; they hadn't bothered with a siren. Maybe somebody called ahead to tell them Mrs. Withers was dead.

Two uniformed policemen questioned Mommy, and then another policeman, in a wrinkled suit and loose tie, talked to Mommy, too. Jessica Ann didn't see him arrive; they were all sitting at tables in the school library now. Jessica Ann was seated by herself, away from them, but she could hear some of the conversation.

The man in the suit and tie was old—probably forty—and he didn't have much hair on the top of his head, though he did have a mustache. He was kind of pudgy and seemed grouchy.

He said to Mommy, "You didn't speak to Mrs. Withers at all?"

"How could I? She was on the floor with her neck broken."

"You had an appointment . . ."

"Yes. A parent/teacher conference. Anything else, Lieutenant March?"

"No. Not right now, ma'am."

"Thank you," Mommy said. She stood. "You have my address, and my number. . . ."

"Yeah," he said. "I got your number."

He was giving Mommy a mean look but she just smiled as she gathered her purse and left.

Soon they were driving home. Mommy was humming a song, but Jessica Ann didn't recognize it. One of the those old songs, from the '80s.

It was funny—her mother didn't seem very upset about Mrs. Withers's accident at all.

But sometimes Mommy was that way about things.

Jessica Ann loved their house on Rockwell Road. It had been built a long time ago—1957, Mommy said—but it was really cool: light brick and dark wood and a lot of neat angles—a split-level ranch-style was how she'd heard her Mommy describe it. They had lived here for two years, ever since Mommy married Mr. Sterling.

Mr. Sterling had been really old—fifty-one, it said in the paper when he died—but Mommy loved him a lot. He had an insurance agency, and was kind of rich—or so they had thought.

She had overheard her Mommy talking to Aunt Beth about it. Aunt Beth was a little older than Mommy, and she was pretty too, but she had dark hair. They reminded Jessica Ann of Betty and Veronica in the *Archie* comic books.

Anyway, one time Jessica Ann heard Mommy in an odd voice, almost a mean voice, complaining that Mr. Sterling hadn't been as rich as he pretended to be. Plus, a lot of his money and property and stuff wound up with his children by (and Mommy didn't usually talk this way, certainly not in front of Jessica Ann) "the first two bitches he was married to."

Still, they had wound up with this cool house.

Jessica Ann missed Mr. Sterling. He was a nice man, before he'd had his heart attack and died. The only thing was, she didn't like having to call him "Daddy." Her real daddy—who died in the boating accident when she was six—was the only one who deserved being called that.

She kept Daddy's picture by her bed and talked to him every night. She remembered him real good—he was a big, handsome man with shoulders so wide you couldn't look at them both at the same time. He was old, too—even older than Mr. Sterling—and had left them "well off" (as Mommy put it).

Jessica Ann didn't know what had happened to Daddy's money—a few times Mommy talked about "bad investments"—but fortunately Mr. Sterling had come along about the time Daddy's money ran out.

When Jessica Ann and her mother got home from the school, Aunt Beth—who lived a few blocks from them, alone, because she was divorced from Uncle Bob—was waiting dinner. Mommy had called her from JFK and asked if she'd help.

As Jessica Ann came in, Aunt Beth was all over her, bending down, putting her arm around her. It made Jessica Ann uneasy. She wasn't used to displays of affection like that—Mommy talked about loving her a lot, but mostly kept her distance.

"You poor dear," Aunt Beth said. "Poor dear." She looked up at Mommy, who was hanging up both their coats in the closet. "Did she see . . . ?"

"No," Mommy said, shutting the closet door. "I discovered the body. Jessica Ann was in the car."

"Thank God!" Aunt Beth said. "Do either of you even feel like eating?"

"I don't know," Jessica Ann said.

"Sure," Mommy said. "Smells like spaghetti."

"That's what it is," Aunt Beth said. "I made a big bowl of salad, too."

"I think I'll go to my room," Jessica Ann said.

"No!" Mommy said. "A little unpleasantness isn't going to stand in the way of proper nutrition."

Aunt Beth was frowning, but it was a sad frown. "Please . . . if she doesn't want . . ."

Mommy gave Aunt Beth the "mind your own business" look. Then she turned to Jessica Ann, and pointed to the kitchen. "Now, march in there, young lady."

"Yes, Mommy."

"Your salad, too."

"Yes, Mommy."

After dinner, Jessica Ann went to her room, a pink world of stuffed animals and Barbie dolls; she had a frilly four-poster bed that Mommy got in an antique shop. She flopped onto it and thought about Mrs. Withers. Thought about what a nice lady Mrs. Withers was. . . .

She was crying into her pillow when Aunt Beth came in.

"There, there," Aunt Beth said, sitting on the edge of the bed, patting the girl's back. "Get it out of your system."

"Do . . . do you think Mrs. Withers had any children?"

"Probably. Maybe even grandchildren."

"Do you . . . do you think I should write them a letter, about what a good teacher she was?"

Aunt Beth's eyes filled up with tears and she clutched Jessica Ann to her. This time Jessica Ann didn't mind. She clutched back, crying into her aunt's blouse.

"I think that's a wonderful idea."

"I'll write it tonight, and add their names later, when I find them out."

"Fine. Jessy . . ." Aunt Beth was the only grown-up who ever called her that; Mommy didn't like nicknames. ". . . you know, your mother . . . she's kind of a . . . special person."

"What do you mean?"

"Well . . . it's just that . . . she has some wonderful qualities."

"She's very smart. And pretty."

"Yes."

"She does everything for me."

"She does a lot for you. But . . . she doesn't always *feel* things like she should."

"What do you mean, Aunt Beth?"

"It's hard to explain. She was babied a lot . . . there were four of us, you know, and she was the youngest. Your grandparents, rest their souls, gave her everything. And why not? She was so pretty, so perfect. . . ."

"She always got her way, didn't she?"

"How did you know that, Jessica Ann?"

"I just do. 'Cause she still does, I guess."

"Jessy . . . I always kind of looked after your mother . . . protected her."

"What do you mean?"

"Just . . . as you grow older, try to understand . . . try to forgive her when she seems . . . if she seems . . ."

"Cold?"

Aunt Beth nodded. Smiled sadly. "Cold," she said. "In her way, she loves you very much."

"I know."

"I have dessert downstairs. You too blue for chocolate cake?"

"Is Mark here? I thought I heard his car."

"He's here," Aunt Beth said, smiling. "And he's asking for you. Mark and chocolate cake—that's quite a combo. . . ."

Jessica Ann grinned, took a tissue from the box on her nightstand, dried her eyes, took her aunt's hand, and allowed herself to be led from her room down the half-stairs.

Mommy's new boyfriend, Mark Jeffries, was in the living room sitting in Mr. Sterling's recliner, sipping an iced tea.

"There's my girl!" he said, as Jessica Ann came into the room; Aunt Beth was in the kitchen with Mommy.

Mark sat forward in the chair, then stood—he was younger than either Mr. Sterling or Daddy, and really good looking, like a soap opera actor with his sandy hair and gray sideburns and deep tan. He wore a green sweater and new jeans and a big white smile. Also, a Rolex watch.

She went quickly to him, and he bent down and hugged her. He smelled good—like lime.

He pushed her gently away and looked at her with concern in his blue-gray eyes. "Are you okay, angel?"

"Sure."

"Your mommy told me about today. Awful rough." He took her by the hand and led her to the couch. He sat down and nodded for her to join him. She did.

"Angel, if you need somebody to talk to . . ."

"I'm fine, Mark. Really."

"You know, when I was ten, my Boy Scout leader died. He was killed in an automobile accident. I didn't have a dad around . . . he and Mom were divorced . . . and my Scout leader was kind of a . . . surrogate father to me. You know what that is?"

"Sure. He kind of took the place of a dad."

"Right. Anyway, when he died, I felt . . . empty. Then I started to get afraid."

"Afraid, Mark?"

"I started to think about dying for the first time. I had trouble. I had nightmares. For the first time I realized nobody lives forever . . ."

Jessica Ann had known that for a long time. First Daddy, then Mr. Sterling. . . .

"I hope you don't have trouble like that," he said.

"But if you do, I just want you to know . . . I'm here for you."

She didn't say anything—just beamed at him.

She was crazy about Mark. Jessica Ann hoped he and Mommy would get married. She thought she could even feel comfortable calling him "Daddy." Maybe.

Mommy had met Mark at a country club dance last month. He had his own business—some kind of mail-order thing that was making a lot of money, she heard Mommy say—and had moved to Ferndale to get away from the "urban blight" where he used to live.

Jessica Ann found she could talk to Mark better than to any grown-up she'd ever met. Even better than Aunt Beth. And as much as Jessica Ann loved her Mommy, they didn't really *talk*—no shared secrets, or problems.

But Mark put Jessica Ann at ease. She could talk to him about problems at school or even at home.

"Who wants dessert?" Aunt Beth called.

Soon Jessica Ann and Mark were sitting at the kitchen table while Mommy, in her perfect white apron (she never got anything on it, so why did she wear it?), was serving up big pieces of chocolate cake.

"I'll just have the ice cream," Aunt Beth told Mommy.

"What's *wrong* with me?" Mommy said. "You're allergic to chocolate! How thoughtless of me."

"Don't be silly . . ."

"How about some strawberry compote on that ice cream?"

"That does sound good."

"There's a jar in the fridge," Mommy said.

Aunt Beth found the jar, but was having trouble opening it.

"Let me have a crack at that," Mark said, and took it, but he must not have been as strong as he looked; he couldn't budge the lid.

"Here," Mommy said impatiently, and took the jar, and with a quick thrust, opened the lid with a loud *pop*. Aunt Beth thanked her and spooned on the strawberry compote herself.

Mommy sure was strong, Jessica Ann thought. She'd seen her do the same thing with ketchup bottles and pickle jars.

"Pretty powerful for a little girl," Mark said teasingly, patting Mommy's rear end when he thought Jessica Ann couldn't see. "Remind me not to cross you."

"Don't cross me," Mommy said, and smiled her beautiful smile.

At school the next day, Jessica Ann was called to the principal's office.

But the principal wasn't there—waiting for her was the pudgy policeman, the one with the mustache. He had on a different wrinkled suit today. He didn't seem so grouchy now; he was all smiles.

"Jessica Ann?" he said, bending down. "Remember me? I'm Lieutenant March. Could we talk for a while?"

"Okay."

"I have permission for us to use Mr. Davis's office. . . ."

Mr. Davis was the principal.

"All right."

Lieutenant March didn't sit at Mr. Davis's desk; he put two chairs facing each other and sat right across from Jessica Ann.

"Jessica Ann, why did your mother want to see Mrs. Withers yesterday?"

"They had a conference."

"Parent/teacher conference."

"Yes, sir."

"You don't have to call me 'sir,' Jessica Ann. I want us to be friends."

She didn't say anything.

He seemed to be trying to think of what to say next; then finally he said, "Do you know how your teacher died?"

"She fell off a ladder."

"She did fall off a ladder. But Jessica Ann—your teacher's neck was broken . . ."

"When she fell off the ladder."

"We have a man called the Medical Examiner who says that it didn't happen that way. He says it's very likely a pair of hands did that."

Suddenly Jessica Ann remembered the jar of strawberry compote, and the other bottles and jars Mommy had twisted caps off, so easily.

"Jessica Ann . . . something was missing from Mrs. Withers's desk."

Jessica Ann's tummy started jumping.

"A plaque, Jessica Ann. A plaque for 'Outstanding Student of the Year.' You won last year, didn't you?"

"Yes, sir."

"Mrs. Withers told several friends that your mother called her, complaining about you not winning this year."

Jessica Ann said nothing.

"Jessica Ann . . . the mother of the boy who won the plaque, Eduardo's mother, Mrs. Melindez, would like to have that plaque. Means a lot to her. If you should happen to find it, would you tell me?"

"Why would *I* find it?"

"You just might. Could your mother have picked it up when she went into the classroom?"

"If she did," Jessica Ann said, "that doesn't prove anything."

"Who said anything about proving anything, Jessica Ann?"

She stood. "I think if you have any more questions for me, Lieutenant March, you should talk to my mother."

"Jessica Ann . . ."

But the little girl didn't hear anything else; not anything the policeman said, or what any of her friends said the rest of the day, or even the substitute teacher.

All she could hear was the sound of the lid on the strawberry compote jar popping open.

* * *

When Jessica Ann got home, she found the house empty. A note from Mommy said she had gone grocery shopping. The girl got herself some milk and cookies but neither drank nor ate. She sat at the kitchen table staring at nothing. Then she got up and began searching her mother's room.

In the middle drawer of a dresser, amid slips and panties, she found the plaque.

Her fingers flew off the object as if it were a burner on a hot stove. Then she saw her own fingerprints glowing on the brass and rubbed them off with a slick pair of panties, and put the shining plaque back, buried it in Mommy's underthings.

She went to her room and found the largest stuffed animal she could and hugged it close; the animal—a bear—had wide button eyes. So did she.

Her thoughts raced; awful possibilities presented themselves, possibilities that she may have already considered, in some corner of her mind, but had banished.

Why did Mr. Sterling die of that heart attack?

What really happened that afternoon Mommy and Daddy went boating?

She was too frightened to cry. Instead she hugged the bear and shivered as if freezing and put pieces together that fit too well. If she was right, then someone *else* she thought the world of was in danger. . . .

Mark Jeffries knew something was wrong, but he couldn't be sure what.

He and Jessica Ann had hit it off from the very start, but for the last week, whenever he'd come over to see her mother, the little girl had avoided and even snubbed him.

It had been a week since the death of Mrs. Withers—he had accompanied both Jessica Ann and her mother to the funeral—and the child had been uncharacteristically brooding ever since.

Not that Jessica Ann was ever talkative: She was a quiet child, intelligent, contemplative even, but when she opened up (as she did for Mark so often) she was warm and funny and fun.

Maybe it was because he had started to stay over at the house, on occasion . . . maybe she was threatened because he had started to share her mother's bedroom. . . .

He'd been lying awake in the mother's bed, thinking these thoughts as the woman slept soundly beside him, when nature called him, and he arose, slipped on a robe, and answered the call. In the hallway, he noticed the little girl's light on in her room. He stopped at the child's room and knocked gently.

"Yes?" came her voice, softly.

"Are you awake, angel?"

"Yes."

He cracked the door. She was under the covers, wide awake, the ruffly pink shade of her nightstand lamp glowing; a stuffed bear was under there with her, hugged to her.

"What's wrong, angel?" he asked, and shut the door behind him, and sat on the edge of her bed.

"Nothing."

"You've barely spoken to me for days."

She said nothing.

"You know you're number one on my personal chart, don't you?"

She nodded.

"Do you not like my sleeping over?"

She shrugged.

"Don't you . . . don't you think I'd make a good daddy?"

Tears were welling in her eyes!

"Angel. . . ."

She burst into tears, clutching him, bawling like the baby she had been not so long ago.

"I . . . I wanted to chase you away."

"Chase me away! Why on earth . . . ?"

"Because . . . because you *would* make a good daddy, and I don't want you to die. . . ."

And she poured it all out, her fears that her mother was a murderer, that Mommy had killed her teacher and her daddy and even Mr. Sterling.

He glanced behind him at the closed door. He gently pushed the girl away and, a hand on her shoulder, looked at her hard.

"How grown-up can you be?" he asked.

"Real grown-up, if I have to."

"Good. Because I want to level with you about something. You might be mad at me . . ."

"Why, Mark?"

"Because I haven't been honest with you. In fact . . . I've lied. . . ."

"Lied?"

And he told her. Told her about being an investigator for the insurance company that was looking into the latest suspicious death linked to her mother, that of her stepfather, Phillip Sterling (at least, the latest one before Mrs. Withers).

Calmly, quietly, he told the little girl that he had come to believe, like her, that her mother was a murderer.

"But you . . . you slept with her . . ."

"It's not very nice. I know. I had to get close to her, to get the truth. With your help, if you can think back and tell me about things you've seen, we might be—"

But that was all he got out.

The door flew open, slapping the wall like a spurned suitor, and there she was, the beautiful little blonde in the baby-doll nightie, a woman with a sweet body that he hadn't been able to resist even though he knew what she most likely was.

There she was with the .38 in her hand and firing at him, again and again; he felt the bullets hitting his body, punching him, burning into him like lasers, he thought, then one entered his right eye and put an end to all thought, and to him.

Jessica Ann was screaming, the bloody body of Mark Jeffries sprawled on the bed before her, scorched bleeding holes on the front of his robe, one of his eyes an awful black hole leaking red.

Mommy sat beside her daughter and hugged her

little girl to her, slipping a hand over her mouth, stifling Jessica Ann's screams.

"Hush, dear. Hush."

Jessica Ann started to choke, and that stopped the screaming, and Mommy took her hand away. The girl looked at her mother and was startled to see tears in Mommy's eyes. She couldn't ever remember Mommy crying, not even at the funerals of Daddy and Mr. Sterling, although she had seemed to cry. Jessica Ann had always thought Mommy was faking . . . that Mommy couldn't cry . . . but now . . .

"We have to call the police, dear," she said, "and when they come, we have to tell them things that fit together. Like a puzzle fits together. Do you understand?"

"Yes, Mommy." Jessica, trembling, wanted to pull away from her mother, but somehow couldn't.

"Otherwise, Mommy will be in trouble. We don't want that, do we?"

"No, Mommy."

"Mark did bad things to Mommy. *Bedroom* things. Do you understand?"

"Yes, Mommy."

"When I heard him in here, I thought he might be doing the same kind of things to you. Or trying to."

"But he didn't—"

"That doesn't matter. And you don't have to say he did. I don't want you to lie. But those things he told you . . . about being an investigator . . . *forget* them. He never said them."

"Oh . . . okay, Mommy."

"If you tell, Mommy would be in trouble. We don't want that."

"No, Mommy."

"Now. Who's your best friend?"

"You . . . you are, Mommy."

"Who loves you more than anything on God's green earth?"

"You do, Mommy."

"Good girl."

There were a lot of men and women in the house, throughout the night, some of them police, in uniform, some of them in white, some in regular clothes, some using cameras, others carrying out Mark in a big black zippered bag.

Lieutenant March questioned Mommy for a long time; when all the others had left, he was still there, taking notes. Mommy sat on a couch in the living room, wearing a robe, her arms folded tight to her, her expression as blank as a doll's. Just behind her was the Christmas tree, in the front window, which Mommy had so beautifully trimmed.

Aunt Beth had been called and sat with Jessica Ann in the kitchen, but there was no doorway, just an archway separating the rooms, so Jessica could see Mommy as Lieutenant March questioned her. Jessica Ann couldn't hear what they were saying most of the time.

Then she saw Mommy smile at Lieutenant March, a funny, making-fun sort of smile, and that seemed to make Lieutenant March angry. He stood and almost shouted.

"No, you're not under arrest," he said, "and yes, you should contact your attorney."

He tromped out to the kitchen with the empty coffee cup (Aunt Beth had given him some) and he looked very grouchy.

"Thank you," he said to Aunt Beth, handing her the cup.

"Don't you believe my sister?" Aunt Beth asked.

"Do you?" He glanced at Jessica Ann, but spoke to Aunt Beth. "I'll talk to the girl tomorrow. Maybe she should stay with you tonight."

"That's not my decision," Aunt Beth said.

"Maybe it should be," he said, and excused himself and left.

Aunt Beth looked very tired when she sat at the table with Jessica Ann. She spoke quietly, almost a whisper.

"What you told me . . . is that what really happened, Jessica Ann?"

"Mommy thought Mark was going to do something bad to me."

"You love your mommy, don't you?"

"Yes."

"But you're also afraid of her."

"Yes." She shrugged. "All kids are afraid of their parents."

"Beth," Mommy said, suddenly in the archway, "you better go now."

Aunt Beth rose. She wet her lips. "Maybe I should take Jessica Ann tonight."

Mommy came over and put her hand on Jessica Ann's shoulder. "We appreciate your concern. But we've been through a lot of tragedy together, Jessica Ann and I. We'll make it through tonight, just fine. Won't we, dear?"

"Yes, Mommy."

Both Jessica Ann and her mother were questioned, individually, at police headquarters in downtown Ferndale the next afternoon. Mommy's lawyer, Mr. Ekhardt, a handsome gray-haired older man, was with them; sometimes he told Mommy not to answer certain questions.

Afterward, in the hall, Jessica Ann heard Mommy ask Mr. Ekhardt if they had enough to hold her.

"Not yet," he said. "But I don't think this is going to let up. From the looks of that lieutenant, I'd say this is just starting."

Mommy touched Mr. Ekhardt's hand with both of hers. "Thank you, Neal. With you in our corner, I'm sure we'll be just fine."

"You never give up, do you?" Mr. Ekhardt said with a funny smile. "Gotta give you that much."

Mr. Ekhardt shook his head and walked away.

Jessica Ann watched as her Mommy pulled suitcases from a closet, and then went to another closet and began packing her nicest things into one of the suitcases.

"We're going on a vacation, dear," Mommy said, folding several dresses over her arm, "to a foreign land—you'll love it there. It'll be Christmas every day."

"But I have school . . ."

"Your break starts next week, anyway. And then we'll put you in a wonderful new school."

"What about my friends?"

"You'll make new friends."

Mommy was packing so quickly, and it was all happening so fast, Jessica Ann couldn't even find the words to protest further. What could she do about it? Every kid knew that when your parents decided to move, the kid had no part of it. A kid's opinion had no weight in such matters. You just went where your parents went.

"Take this," Mommy said, handing her the smaller suitcase, "and pack your own things."

"What about my animals?"

"Take your favorite. Aunt Beth will send the others on later."

"Okay, Mommy."

"Who's your best friend?"

"You are."

"Who loves you more than—"

"You do."

The girl packed her bag. She put the framed picture of Daddy in the middle of the clothes, so it wouldn't get broken.

* * *

They drove for several hours. Mommy turned the radio on to a station playing Christmas music—"White Christmas" and the one about chestnuts roasting. Now and then Mommy looked over at her, and Jessica Ann noticed Mommy's expression was . . . different. Blank, but Mommy's eyes seemed . . . was Mommy frightened, too?

When Mommy noticed Jessica Ann had caught her gaze, Mommy smiled that beautiful smile. But it wasn't real. Jessica Ann wasn't sure Mommy knew how to *really* smile.

The motel wasn't very nice. It wasn't like the Holiday Inns and Marriotts and Ramada Inns they usually stayed in on vacation. It was just a white row of doorways on the edge of some small town and a junkyard was looming in back of it, like some scary Disneyland.

Jessica Ann put on her jammies and brushed her teeth and Mommy tucked her in, even gave her a kiss. The girl was very, very tired and fell asleep quickly.

She wasn't sure how long she'd been asleep, but when she woke up, Mommy was sitting on the edge of Jessica Ann's bed. Mommy wasn't dressed for bed; she still had on the clothes she'd been driving in.

Mommy was sitting there, in the dark, staring, her hands raised in the air. It was like Mommy was trying to choke a ghost.

"Sometimes mommys have to make hard decisions," Mommy whispered. "If they take Mommy away, who would look after you?"

But Jessica Ann knew Mommy wasn't saying this to her, at least not to the awake her. Maybe to the sleeping Jessica Ann, only Jessica Ann wasn't sleeping. . . .

The child bolted out of the bed with a squealing scream and Mommy ran after her. Jessica Ann got to the door, which had a night latch, but her fingers fumbled with the chain, and then her Mommy was on top of her. Mommy's hands were on her, but the child squeezed through and bounded over one of the twin beds and ran into the bathroom and slammed and locked the door.

"Mommy! Mommy, don't!"

"Let me in, Jessica Ann. You just had a bad dream. Just a nightmare. We'll go back to sleep now."

"No!"

The child looked around the small bathroom and saw the window; she stood on the toilet-seat lid and unlocked the window and slipped out, onto the tall grass. Behind her, she heard the splintering of the door as her mother pushed it open.

Jessica Ann was running, running toward the dark shapes that were the junkyard; she glanced back and saw her mother's face framed in the bathroom window. Her mother's eyes were wild; Jessica Ann had never seen her mother like that.

"Come back here this *instant*!" her mother said.

But Jessica Ann ran, screaming as she went, hoping to attract attention. The moon was full and high and like a spotlight on the child. Maybe someone would see!

"Help! Please, help!"

Her voice seemed to echo through the night. The other windows in the motel were dark and the highway out front was deserted; there was no one else in the world but Jessica Ann and Mommy.

And Mommy was climbing out the bathroom window.

Jessica Ann climbed over the wire fence—there was some barbed wire at the top, and her jammies got caught and tore a little, but she didn't cut herself. Then she was on the other side, in the junkyard, but her bare feet hurt from the cinders beneath them.

Mommy was coming.

The child ran, hearing the rattle of the fence behind her, knowing Mommy was climbing, climbing over, then dropping to the other side. . . .

"Jessica Ann."

Piles of crushed cars were on either side of Jessica Ann, as she streaked down a cinder path between them, her feet hurting, bleeding, tears streaming, her crying mixed with gasping for air as she ran, ran hard as she could.

Then she fell and she skinned her knee and her yelp echoed.

She got up quickly, and ran around the corner, and ran right into her mother.

"What do you think you're doing, young lady?"

Her mother's hands gripped the girl's shoulders.

Jessica Ann backed up, bumping into a rusted-out

steel drum. A wall of crushed cars, scrap metal, old tires, broken-down appliances, and other things that must have had value once was behind her.

"Mommy . . ."

Mommy's hands were like claws reaching out for the girl's neck. "This is for your own good, dear. . . ."

Then Mommy's hands were on Jessica Ann's throat, and the look in Mommy's eyes was so very cold, and the child tried to cry out but she couldn't, though she tried to twist away and moonlight fell on her face.

Mommy gazed at her child, and her eyes narrowed and softened, and she loosened her hands.

"Put your hands *up*, Mrs. Sterling!"

Mommy stepped away and looked behind her. Jessica Ann, touching her throat where Mommy had been choking her, could see him standing there, Lieutenant March. He was pointing a gun at Mommy.

Mommy put her head down and her hands up.

Then Aunt Beth was there, and took Jessica Ann into her arms and held her, and said, "You're a brave little girl."

"What . . . what are you *doing* here, Aunt Beth?"

"I went along with the lieutenant. He was keeping your mother under surveillance. I'm glad you have good lungs, or we wouldn't have heard you back here. We were out front, and I'd fallen asleep. . . ."

"Aunt Beth . . . can I live with you now? I don't want to go to a new school."

Aunt Beth's laugh was surprised and sort of sad.

"You can live with me. You can stay in your school." She stroked Jessica Ann's forehead. "It's over now, Jessy. It's over."

"She couldn't do it, Aunt Beth," Jessica Ann said, crying, but feeling strangely happy, somehow. Not to be rescued, but to know Mommy couldn't bring herself to do it! Mommy couldn't kill Jessica Ann!

"I know, honey," Aunt Beth said, holding the girl.

"Mommy *does* love me! More than anything on God's green earth."

The child didn't hear when Lieutenant March, cuffing her hands behind her, asked the woman, "Why didn't you do it? Why'd you hesitate?"

"For a moment there, in the moonlight," Mommy said, "she looked like *me*. . . ."

And the cop walked the handcuffed woman to his unmarked car, while the aunt took her niece into the motel room to retrieve a stuffed bear and a framed photo of Daddy.

The author on his ultimate fear . . .

My biggest fear doesn't have a name. It is tied to a character trait of mine—or possibly flaw—perhaps best demonstrated by the fact that I still live in the small town I was born and raised in, forty-some years ago, and that at age twenty, I married my childhood sweetheart to whom I am still blissfully wed.

Possibly the best term for this form of dread is fear of change. It's a fear that my world will be taken out from under me—that my lifeline will be cut, my security will be lost. It is this fear that makes us cower before sadistic, unreasonable bosses—the parental figures of our careers.

And, so, it all goes back to that truly primal fear: fear of your parents. Fear of the punishment, the wrath of those who gave you life, those who sheltered you, shaped and controlled you. Or even worse, the fear of losing them. . . .

You don't have to have been abused (and I certainly wasn't—I was if anything pampered) to understand this basic fear. If there wasn't some truth to what I'm saying, then who among the grown-ups reading this has never shared with a mate or a confidant the startling news that one or both of your parents is driving you crazy?

MOMMY'S LITTLE HELPERS

This story began several years ago, as a fleeting idea I discussed with my wife, writer Barbara Collins, on a Sunday afternoon outing; it reflects a love of a kind of story more common to the '40s and '50s than today, in which the question of evil is discussed in rather genteel terms—typified by such films as Alfred Hitchcock's *Shadow of a Doubt* (from a Thornton Wilder story), John Stahl's *Leave Her to Heaven* (from the Ben Ames Williams novel), and especially Mervyn LeRoy's *The Bad Seed* (from William March's brilliant novel and Maxwell Anderson's faithful play).

My short story "Mommy" first appeared in *Fear Itself* (Warner Books, 1995), edited by Jeff Gelb, whom I thank for giving this project its official start.

My screenplay, *Mommy,* was written especially for actress Patty McCormack, after she responded favorably to an advance look at the short story. Patty, of course, portrayed the evil child Rhoda Penmark in both the classic Broadway play and the Hollywood film *The Bad Seed.* In 1994, on money raised locally, I wrote, directed, and executive-produced *Mommy* in my hometown, Muscatine, Iowa; an independent film with a budget of under $1 million, *Mommy* was designed for home video and cable, where it currently resides.

Early on in the *Mommy* movie project, I began to think about the possibility of doing a novel version of the story—not a novelization (an odious word for a difficult and thankless task, by the way), but an extension and fleshing out of material in the short story and the screenplay. What particularly interested me was the notion of beginning with what would in effect be a prequel to the story and film. And perhaps, as a novelist-turned-filmmaker, I couldn't consider the project complete until it was a book.

Without the warm critical and public reception our little film has received, this novel might not have been possible; in that vein, an early supporter of *Mommy,* Leonard Maltin, deserves mention and thanks here. So do Donald E. Westlake, Lawrence Block, John Lutz, and Warren Murphy, all of whom championed the film.

While this novel stands alone (just as the film does, and the short story), I must thank the wonderful actors—Michael Cornelison, Jason Miller, Brinke Stevens, Majel Barrett, Sarah Jane Miller, Mickey Spillane, and especially Mommy and Jessica Ann, that is, Patty McCormack and Rachel Lemieux—whose characterizations I carried with me into the writing of this novel.

To these names I must add Phil Dingeldein, Steve Henke, Richard Lowry, and of course my wife, Barb, who were among my main collaborators on the movie *Mommy.* To see the names of the others to whom I owe thanks, you will need to rent the movie *Mommy* and study the end credits. I suggest you do that as soon as possible...and then rent *Mommy 2: Mommy's Day,* for the rest of the story...until the novel comes out.

ATTENTION
WESTERN
CUSTOMERS!
SPECIAL
TOLL-FREE NUMBER
1-800-481-9191
Call Monday through Friday
12 noon to 10 p.m.
Eastern Time
Get a free catalogue,
join the Western Book Club,
and order books using your
Visa, MasterCard,
or Discover®
Leisure
Books